LOVE LOST AND THEN FOUND IN THE CIVIL WAR

By

WILLIAM TIRRE

TABLE OF CONTENTS

ABOUT THE AUTHOR

"William (Bill) Tirre resides in Fairfax, Virginia, with his wife. Empty-nesters, their three grown sons are forging their own paths in their respective careers. Bill's journey began in Saint Louis, known as the Gateway to the West. He pursued higher education at Saint Louis University, Illinois State University, and the University of Illinois, ultimately earning a Ph.D. in educational psychology. His professional life includes nineteen years of service at the National Center for Education Statistics, a branch of the U.S. Department of Education. Prior to this, he contributed five years to the Ball Foundation in suburban Chicago and seventeen years at the Air Force Research Laboratory in San Antonio, Texas.

In his leisure time, Bill enjoys reading, writing, basketball, and pickleball. A devout Christian, he actively participates in Bible studies for adults at his church and has previously led similar studies. Now, in retirement, Bill is dedicated to writing westerns and science fiction, with four published books to his name. Readers can expect to find his faith intricately woven into his stories."

INTRODUCTION

"In this gripping story, Simon and Josiah flee Virginia's turmoil for the promise of freedom in Canada during the Civil War. Their unyielding friendship and deepening faith guide them through treacherous trials and unexpected romances.

Simon, a 24-year-old graduate of the Lutheran seminary in Gettysburg, and 19-year-old Josiah, a slave on a Virginia plantation, embark on a perilous journey north. As they travel, their bond strengthens, with Simon mentoring Josiah, whose growing faith helps him endure numerous hardships, eventually becoming a devout believer.

Simon had been engaged to Emily, a planter's daughter, but her father forces her to end the engagement when Simon refuses to join the Confederate Army. Josiah, a quadroon, is the illegitimate son of the planter and his mulatto housekeeper, a secret known only to them.

To avoid service in the Confederate Army, Simon heads to Canada, with Josiah seeking freedom by his side. Their journey is fraught with danger and challenges, but they also find love. Simon meets Gabrielle, an escaped slave, at a Quaker farm, where he recovers after slave hunters attack him and abduct Josiah. Two Indian men rescue Josiah, reuniting him with Simon at the farm, a stop on the Underground Railroad. Later in Ohio, Josiah meets and falls in love with 17-year-old Justine, who is half Wyandotte Indian.

Gabrielle, initially believed to be one of the Quaker family's daughters, is actually an octoroon girl who escaped sexual slavery.

She blends into the Quaker family, who invite her to stay. Despite her past, she eventually overcomes her fears and falls in love with Simon, with the support of her adoptive Quaker family. Justine, raised in a loving Christian home, receives wholehearted approval from her family for her relationship with Josiah.

Reaching Chatham, Ontario, Simon and Josiah start a successful cobbling business. However, both are eventually drawn to join the war effort. Simon enlists as a Union chaplain, and after meeting Frederick Douglass, Josiah joins an all-black Massachusetts infantry regiment. In his first battle, Josiah is captured and sold back into slavery in Virginia. He escapes but faces his former captor, the slave hunter, who intends to kill him".

CHAPTER ONE

Simon Albrecht, 24, a freshly minted graduate of Lutheran Seminary at Gettysburg, sat at the dinner table of Mr. and Mrs. Henry Lee Howell, parents of his fiancée, Emily (22), a petite redhead with long flowing locks and green eyes. Simon was a slender and handsome young man with dark blonde hair and blue eyes. At five feet nine inches, he was average in height. The Howell home was located on a plantation near Middleburg, Virginia, which had been held by the Howell family for several generations. Henry Lee Howell affected aristocratic airs and, in fact, was something of an aristocrat in Loudon County because of his wealth and his ancestor, American Revolutionary War Lieutenant Colonel and Virginia statesman, Lawrence Howell. In contrast, Simon was from a family of more modest means, the son of Johannes and Maria Albrecht of Culpeper Virginia, near the original German colony in Virginia, Fort Germanna, which dated back to 1714. The Albrecht family first made their living as shoemakers, but in a few generations branched out and became merchants who owned and operated a dry goods store. But Opa Albrecht never let anyone forget how they started – he had a sign posted in the store that said, "We have not forgotten our roots – we still will make you your boots."

It was Saturday, May 25, 1861, and news of the secession of Virginia from the Union by referendum on May 23 was the topic of many discussions. A war between the North and South was imminent with the bombardment of Fort Sumter in the port of Charleston by the South Carolina militia. The soldiers in the fort did not return fire until after two hours of bombardment had transpired. An unarmed supply ship, the Star of the West, had been turned away by militia fire, and so the battle for Fort Sumter took on the character of a siege. President Lincoln had dispatched warships to help defend the fort, but they arrived too late. Major Robert Anderson, commander of the Union garrison, formally surrendered the fort to Confederate General Beauregard at 2:30 p.m., April 13. No soldiers on either side were killed during the battle.

The topic of discussion at the dinner table that evening was the secession of most southern states, now including Virginia, from the Union and the declaration of war. "It is a new declaration of independence!" cried Henry Lee. His wife, Martha, responded, "Oh, must you talk about this most recent unpleasantness at the dinner table, Henry?"

"My dear, the Yankees are threatening our way of life, if not our very existence, with that radical Republican in office. And Mr. Lincoln has called for an army of 75,000 men to invade the sovereign commonwealth of Virginia and other southern states and to subjugate us! What does Mr. Lincoln propose to do with these thousands, no I daresay millions of slaves who are incapable of leading productive and independent lives as freemen? As any reasonable man knows, they need the protection and guidance of the white man to survive in the civilized world! And always remember that, left to their own devices, the colored man reverts to his natural state, which is little more than an animal. Horrible atrocities were committed during the Nat Turner Rebellion of 1831 – these were the actions of a species incapable of moral reasoning!"

Terribly embarrassed, Martha and Emily looked down at their plates, no doubt hoping that Henry Lee would cease this impolite tirade. Simon was suffering in silence, struggling to hold back the obvious retorts that white Americans deliberately outlawed the education of slaves, thereby limiting their ability to succeed on their own, and that for months after the slave rebellion, whites committed their own atrocities against Black people, slave or freeman.

Henry Lee paused for dramatic effect and looked around the table. Then, with no little pride announced, "I am pleased to announce that I have accepted a commission as a colonel in the Army of Northern Virginia, which is being formed to repel the Northern aggressors."

Martha burst into tears and said, "Henry Lee, you will end up getting yourself killed in this terrible war!"

"Martha, Martha – we will win this war in less than ninety days. I could be home for the corn harvest!" But Martha was not mollified, and she hastily left the dining room.

Henry Lee then turned his attention to Simon, "Simon, young man, have you given thought to enlisting in the Army of Northern Virginia?" His tone was not friendly.

Simon was hoping he would not be asked this question, but he had resolved to answer it truthfully because that seemed to be the Christian thing to do. It was part of his Christian witness.

"Well, sir, I have given much thought and prayer to this issue, and I feel compelled to say that I cannot in conscience fight for the continuation of slavery in the United States."

Henry Lee's face darkened, "Those damned Yankees at Gettysburg have filled your head with all kinds of abolitionist notions! Why, you have even picked up their manner of speaking during your four years of schooling up there. Now, here's something I'll bet those fancy professors didn't teach you: Jesus, not once in his lifetime, spoke against slavery!"

Mr. Howell, what you say is likely true, at least from what is recorded in the Bible; but it is not the entire truth. Jesus neither condemned nor condoned slavery. In his day, slavery, as practiced by the Romans and Greeks, was quite different from what we have in our society today. Slaves were not regarded as inferior human beings who existed just to serve White people, to do their heavy labor and dirty work. The majority of slaves were White people taken captive during Roman conquests. In fact, many slaves were taken from southern Slavic countries. The word "Slav" gave rise to "slave". Sometimes, Greek slaves were educated and were given the duty of tutoring the sons of well-to-do Romans in Greek, mathematics, and logic. And before the Christian era, during Old Testament times…"

"Enough already!" Henry Lee almost growled, glaring at Simon. And then mockingly, "I suppose you still want to put all that book learning to use as a pastor, but no church has called you, have they? So, how do you propose to make a living? Become a schoolteacher?

"I suppose I could become a schoolteacher or perhaps a shoemaker like my ancestors," Simon offered. "Of course, Jesus himself was a tradesman (a carpenter) until age 30 when he began his public ministry."

"No Howell daughter has married a tradesman in a hundred years! Just get that notion out of your head now."

"Simon, nearly all the young men in Virginia will be enlisting in the Confederate Army or Navy, and after the war, the young men who served their country will have the first pick of jobs. No man can shirk his duties to the Commonwealth and not expect consequences."

"Sir, my first duty is to God, and He has called me to be a man of peace and a man who seeks justice for the oppressed. Serving in the Confederate Army would not be consistent with what I am called to do."

Henry Lee sat back in his chair and stared at Simon for some seconds, "Well, young man, it is time for you to go home now. I will think about what you have said this evening. If I see a future for you in this family, I will let you know."

Emily said, "But Papa…" Henry Lee cut her off, "Emily, you are the prettiest girl in Loudon County and perhaps the wealthiest. It is time for you to reconsider your engagement."

Simon left the Howell residence and walked to the livery stable. As he approached the building, the stable boy, Josiah (18), appeared, leading Simon's horse out. He was followed by the housekeeper, Nancy De Mornay, who was his mother. They were Black slaves despite their light complexions, signaling significant Caucasian ancestry. They were Black enough by Virginia law.

"Massa Albrecht, I knew you were coming, so I got your horse ready for you. But before you leave, we got somethin to say to you."

Nancy chimed in, "Simon, we overheard your conversation with Massa Howell, and we thank you for standing up to the Massa and being true to your faith. Are you truly an abolitionist and want to free the slaves?"

"Yes, I am certainly in favor of abolition, but I haven't been actively pursuing it."

"What are you going to do now? Massa Howell is gonna force Miss Emily to break off the engagement – you know that, don't you?"

"Yes, there is little doubt about that. But I want to give Emily a chance to elope with me. Maybe she will agree to meet with me where we can discuss this. I want to see if she will escape this war with me and go to Canada to start a new life together there. Slavery is outlawed there, which I think is what Christ would want."

"Oh child, you can try, but I don't think Miss Emily will give up all her fancy clothes, servants, and cotillions. She was brought up thinking of herself as an aristocrat who is entitled to all these things. And her daddy might disinherit her! I can tell her of your plan but…"

"I know, I might be asking too much of her to turn her back on the only life she knows."

Josiah looked like he was going to burst with a question he had for Simon.

"Massa Albrecht, you are planning to go to Canada? Sir, I want to go with you! I want to be a free man! There are some Black towns in Canada that escaped slaves founded, and I want to move there."

"Hmm, perhaps you could accompany me posing as my manservant. This is a common practice, and no one would suspect that you are a runaway slave."

"Hey, much better to travel with you as your manservant than go to war with my father."

"Your father?" asked Simon.

Nancy explained, "Massa Howell is Josiah's father. Massa Howell told us he wants to take Josiah with him as a manservant when he becomes an officer in the Confederate army."

"I would be helping the Confederate cause and hindering the freedom of my own people – that would not be right!"

Simon was taken aback by the revelation of Josiah's father. "Then you are Emily's half-brother and are half-White."

Nancy responded, "Josiah is actually three-fourths White, because I am half White myself."

"So, the irony is that it seems even if you are mostly White, if you have just one drop of Black blood, you will be considered Black and can be kept as a slave. Does anyone in the Howell family know that you, Josiah, are the son of Henry Lee?"

"As far as I know, only Massa Howell knows that I am his son."

"Listen, I'm formulating a plan – I'm going to need some time to get ready for this trip. So, let's say that in two weeks, I come here at first light with a buckboard wagon and two horses. We'll travel northwest to Lake Erie, where I'm hoping we can catch a ferry to

Chatham, Ontario, Canada. This town is the northern terminus for the Underground Railroad, and I've heard that a lot of runaway slaves have settled there and are making good lives for themselves."

"How far is Chatham from here?"

"It's about a 460-mile journey or about 14 days. We'll need to bring a two-man tent, some cookware, and some money. I think I'll just withdraw my life's savings from the bank because it's likely I won't be returning here for quite some time. We don't know how long this war between the states will last and in what shape the South will be when it is over."

"Which side do you think is gonna win this war?"

Simon was silent for a few seconds and then said, "Ultimately, I think the North will win if this turns out to be an extended war because the North has the factories to build the machines, arms, and ammunition needed to equip an army. The North wants to preserve the Union so it won't give up easily. Of course, I'm sad to say most Whites in the North don't care one way or the other if Blacks are slaves or free, so they might not fight hard, and that's to the South's advantage. The South has passion on its side – leaders here in the South are already seeing this as a war of Northern aggression, never mind the fact that the South fired the first shots. Southerners will see themselves as defenders of their homes and families, so I expect the South to fight to the last man. The North just doesn't have the passion needed to end this war quickly. But in the end, the North will win, and much of the South will be laid waste, especially here in Virginia."

Josiah's enthusiasm appeared to wane momentarily when he thought of something.

"Massa Albrecht, sir, I ain't got no fancy dress-up clothes like the house servants wear. And I ain't got no socks and shoes! How can I pass as your manservant?"

"I will pack some spare clothes for you. We are about the same size. They should fit. Shoes could be a problem because your feet are bigger than mine. Say, I've got an idea – my grandfather trained me in the skills of a shoemaker. I'll make you a pair of shoes – can you get permission to visit my home in Middleburg on Wednesday so I can measure your feet?"

"Yes, I often drive Miss Emily to the church on Wednesdays. So maybe we can meet then."

Mrs. De Mornay spoke to Emily in little more than a whisper, "Miss Emily, Massa Simon aksed me to tell you he wants to meet with you in person. He knows that he can't be comin around here anymore. He wants to meet you in the town when you make your usual trip to the church for the ladies' Bible study on Wednesday afternoon. He says you will know the place."

"Oh, Mrs. De Mornay, please tell Simon I will meet with him as he requests."

Wednesday afternoon came, and Josiah drove the carriage around the circular drive to the front porch of the Georgian-style mansion of the Howell family. Josiah helped Miss Emily into the carriage and then drove the four miles to the village of Middleburg.

"Josiah, I am going to meet with a friend briefly before I go to the church. Will you please drop me off at the Red Fox Inn?"

"Yes, Miss Emily. And den, I can drive you over to the church as usual."

Upon arrival, Josiah helped Miss Emily down from the carriage. Then, he drove off to park the rig elsewhere.

Behind the Inn, there was a short gravel trail through the woods. Emily walked the trail until she came upon a park bench and sat down. Two minutes later, Simon appeared and sat down on the bench beside her.

"Simon, before you say anything, please forgive my father for the rude treatment you received from him. My mother and I are quite embarrassed. But I also need to say that my father has ordered me to break off our engagement. He is rather adamant about this," she said with eyes glistening with tears.

"Well, as I see it, we have three possible courses of action." Emily sat back, somewhat dumbfounded.

"When my father gives an order, he expects it to be followed."

"Yes, I know as much – but please listen – here are our options. One, we can break off our engagement and never see each other again, which I guess is what your father would want. Two, we can wait until the war ends and then attempt the engagement again. I think by then, your father will realize the foolishness of the war when the South loses and there is widespread destruction of the South. And three, you can elope with me to Canada, and I mean soon before the war heats up. I love you and want to marry you. We would start a new life together there, away from this horrible war in a new country where no person is enslaved."

Emily sat there and cried. "Simon, I want you to know that I love you, but I can't elope with you. My father would disinherit me, and my mother would be alone in that big house. And what if my father is killed during the war? I won't leave her alone as a widow. No, I have a responsibility to my mother."

"Then do you want to end our relationship now, just as your father dictates?"

With some hesitancy, Emily said, "No…, I don't want to give up on you. You are a fine, noble man who truly practices his faith. This is a deception, but I want to tell my father that our engagement is broken, but in secret, we will maintain our promise to each other until the end of the war. Will you be leaving Middleburg? If so, where will you go?"

"Please keep this confidential, but I am leaving the United States for Chatham, Canada. It is the terminus for the underground railroad and hundreds if not thousands of escaped slaves have settled there. They need teachers and pastors there, and I can fulfill either role. It seems that this is what God is calling me to do. When one door is closed, He opens another."

"Simon, how long will this war last? My father thinks it will be all over in 90 days."

"I think your father is sorely mistaken because this is a watershed moment for the United States. If the South wins the war and the union cannot be maintained, then the greatest attempt at a constitutional republic the world may ever see will be ruined, and freedom will be stricken a terrible blow. Lincoln would rather die than see that happen. Of course, if the North wins, the abolishment of slavery would bring radical changes to Southern society. Plantation owners such as your father would have to pay their field hands and house staff regular wages. The plantation economy will cease to be viable. To be honest, I am expecting this war will last years, not months. Both sides have too much to lose."

Emily sat there on the bench, wiping her tears. "These are horrible times, Simon, and I wish I could spend them at your side. I will wait for you. Please wait for me!"

Simon then took Emily into his arms and kissed her. She passively, but not passionately, returned the kiss. She loved Simon, but she was beginning to question whether she could give up the privileges she had enjoyed as the daughter of a prominent Virginia family or live with discord in the Howell family because she had married a man below her social stratum who was disloyal to Virginia.

CHAPTER TWO

Ingrid Albrecht noted that Simon appeared to be busy gathering materials and packing as if he were preparing for a long road trip. That evening at dinner (Simon was staying with his parents, Johannes and Ingrid, in their home above the store), Ingrid asked Simon directly, "Simon, are you planning a long trip or actually leaving home for good? I could not help but notice all this activity recently buying a small buckboard wagon, a two-man tent, cooking pots and pans, and two mules. We realize that you are a grown man, Simon, but when were you going to tell your parents what your plans are?"

"Well, Mother, I suppose this is the time for me to announce my plans. But first, let me give you some background on what has happened in my life this past week."

"Mr. Howell forced Emily to break off our engagement because I said I would not join the Confederate cause. I explained that slavery was not consistent with my Christian faith, and I would not fight to preserve slavery."

Johannes, Simon's father, pressed back into his chair and said, "I'm sorry, son, that your engagement ended this way. But as your Uncle Fritz once told me, there will be another stagecoach tomorrow morning that will take you where you want to go. I'm sure that your refusal to join the Army of Northern Virginia went over well with old Howell, seeing as he owns about thirty slaves!"

"He announced that he was being commissioned as a colonel in the Army of Northern Virginia and was forming a volunteer regiment."

Johannes snickered and said, "Henry Lee Howell has as much military experience as the typical milk cow and far less courage! If the Confederate Army is going to be led by politically appointed officers, I don't see how they can win. But I don't doubt that there will be some of that going on with the Union army as well."

"Father, I expect that with union armies marching through Virginia, there will be many battles and skirmishes on Virginia soil. The Union Army will want to capture Richmond, and there are only about 100 miles between Washington City and Richmond, the proposed new Confederate capital. Moving the capital will be a mistake that costs the Confederacy a victory. The situation will quickly become ugly. Agriculture and business will be disrupted."

"Can we change the subject? I am so tired of this talk of war!" said Ingrid.

"Simon, I never brought this up with you before, but did you ever think you would fit in with the Howell's social circle? You weren't raised as a privileged aristocrat, and you know that the Albrecht family (and my family of birth, the Schmidts) never owned a single slave. From the beginning, we found slavery to be abhorrent. Emily is a sweet girl, but she has never even cooked, cleaned, or sewn in all her life. All this was done for her."

"Mother, I admit that there were going to be some differences in backgrounds that we would have to deal with as a married couple, but I love the girl, and she loves me. That should be enough."

"Well, the biggest problem is that old windbag, Henry Lee himself, as your recent experience showed," Johannes said. "Remember, when you marry a girl, you are also marrying into a family. Can you imagine life as the son-in-law of that phony aristocrat? Would you want your children to be subjected to a man of his character as their maternal grandfather?"

Simon was silent for a few seconds as he studied his dinner plate, "No, I had not really given much thought to these issues."

"So, back to our first question, what exactly are you planning to do?"

"Well, Father, if I stay here, it is likely that people will try to pressure me into joining the Army of Northern Virginia. If I refuse, I might be branded as a coward and never be called by a church, at least in Virginia. I can't let that happen. My plan is to escape the war by moving to Canada, where there is no slavery, and work as either a schoolteacher, a pastor, or maybe even as a cobbler. I will stay in Canada for at least the duration of this foolish war."

"If you don't want to fight for the independence of the Southern states and the continuation of slavery, why not volunteer with the Union army and fight for the elimination of slavery?"

"For a very simple reason – I don't want to fight against my neighbors and friends I grew up with here in Virginia. I don't necessarily hate anyone who wants to defend slavery – I much rather persuade such folks to see how slavery is immoral and how it is irrational and ultimately destructive to the South to continue enslaving colored people."

Simon's father gave a slight nod of understanding and leaned back in his chair. Simon's mother, Ingrid, was concerned about the embarrassment Simon's absence would cause, almost whining, "Simon, what can we say to our neighbors, friends, and customers about your absence? Our business depends on the good will of our customers – what if they think we have raised an ungrateful, disloyal coward and stay away from our store?"

Simon chafed at his mother's choice of words.

Did these words come so easily to her because that is how she thinks of me?

"Mother, you and Father raised me to believe that my faith should permeate my life and be reflected in all I think, say, and do. There never was the promise that living one's life as a Christian would be easy. Nor was there any promise of popularity. If you think it would help, I can write an explanation for my departure and absence that you can give to anyone who questions you or post in a public place for all to see."

"Print it in large letters, Simon, and I will post it on the inside of our display window," said Johannes. We have nothing to be ashamed of. No, we have every good reason to be proud of you!"

"Thank you, father. Now, I must excuse myself from the table. I have some shoes to make."

When Simon had walked out of sight, Ingrid said quietly, "Oh, but must you be so Christian?"

Simon was meeting with Josiah so that Josiah could try on his new shoes.

"Before you try on your shoes, slip into these socks. You'll be wearing socks and shoes on our trip."

Josiah pulled on the socks and tried on the shoes. He was surprised by how they felt and tried to walk in them. "Oh, it's gonna take some time to get used to these shoes! My feet feel so trapped."

"Do your toes have enough room, or are they pinched on the sides? And what about your big toe – when you push forward, do you feel your big toe hitting the front of the shoe?"

"No, they don't pinch, and I don't feel the front of the shoe."

"Then it looks like you are good to go. Will you be able to start our journey the day after tomorrow? You remember where our meeting place will be, right? And that we must leave at first light?"

"Yes, sir! And I'm not to carry anything with me because you will be providing my new clothing appropriate for a gentleman's manservant."

"Oh, but sir – what protection will we have against highwaymen and slave catchers?

"I will have a Colt 1851 Navy revolver that I bought in Alexandria that should persuade highwaymen not to bother us. If not so persuaded, well, I may be a peace-loving man up to a point – but I won't allow anyone to harm us with a gun or knife – no, I will fight back. As for protection against fugitive slave catchers, I have forged a certificate that says you are a freeman. But here is something I just learned the other day – freeborn people of color are allowed to reside in Virginia, but slaves who have been freed by their masters must move out of the commonwealth. So, if we are stopped by a slave patrol, I will show them your certificate of freedom, and if they have any intention of following the law, they will let us proceed without hassle."

"Massa Simon, seems you done thought of everything!"

"Josiah, remember – don't call me master! We don't want anyone to think right away that you were ever a slave. We'll only show someone your certificate of freedom if we are asked to produce it."

CHAPTER THREE

Before sunrise one Sunday, Simon quietly left his parents' home and hitched up the mules he had purchased to his buckboard wagon. His shoemaker's toolbox was already loaded, as was his cookware, the two-man tent, and various books, including his Bible and some commentaries. Two carpetbags held clothes for Josiah and himself. He drove to the pre-arranged meeting place where he was to pick up Josiah. Josiah was already waiting when Simon arrived.

"Josiah, you remembered not to tell any one of our plans that we were leaving this Sunday morning – that included your mother, right?"

Josiah answered, "No Sir, I didn't tell nobody. When they wakes up this morning they will be surprised they don't see me nowhere."

"Good," said Simon, "I didn't tell my parents either. They will be surprised but they knew it was coming. They knew I was going to move to Canada to flee this war and to start a new life there. Josiah, we must prepare you for living as an independent and productive member of society. I suspect there are a lot of things that weren't taught to slaves because it was assumed you would continue as a slave the rest of your life."

"With that in mind, did anyone teach you how to read and do arithmetic?"

"Yes, my half-sister taught me some, not knowing I was her kin."

"Well, I was thinking that we could pick up where Emily left off. This is important because, in the colonies of free Black men in Canada, you will find work quicker if you have these skills. And we will need to work on your speech habits. You don't want to sound like a slave! Stop referring to me as Master, enunciate your words clearly, and look people in the eye when you are speaking to them. You don't need to look down at your feet with a submissive attitude."

"Well, don't I know it! Maybe you can teach me how to make shoes too. Say, what are you planning to do? Are you going to be a shoemaker, a teacher, or a preacher man?"

Simon laughed, "Well, for a while, I might try to do all three. We'll have to see what opportunities there are in Chatham. Of course, I could always make and repair shoes as a sideline, and you could apprentice under me. We'll just have to wait and see."

Simon and Josiah sat on the buckboard pulled by Simon's two mules, Ruth and Naomi. They traveled at about three miles per hour for about ten hours each day. It was about 380 miles to Sandusky, Ohio, on the shore of Lake Eerie, so they had a long journey ahead of them.

On this first day of travel, which was a Sunday, they had no trouble until around 2:00 o'clock in the afternoon when they saw three rather rough-looking characters riding toward them. Simon felt his heart begin to pound in his chest – these ruffians were no doubt slave catchers, and they were now blocking the road! Simon brought his mules to a halt, and in a normal and confident voice as he could muster, he said, "Good afternoon, gentlemen. Is there something I can help you with?"

"Well, ain't you the polite one! We are law enforcement officers, and it is our duty to catch runaway slaves and bring them back to their masters where they belong! Right now, we're hunting down a pair of niggers – a huge buck, black as coal, and a girl described as a yellow rose, that he fancies as his wife. They escaped from a plantation in North Carolina about five days ago." The spokesperson for this patrol was their leader, who hadn't seen a bathtub in many days and possibly never a toothbrush. If he didn't start brushing soon, he was going to miss the opportunity.

The leader of these slave catchers frowned as he scrutinized Josiah. Then he grunted and said,

"If ah'm not mistaken, and ah'm rarely mistaken, this boy heah is one of them pale-skinned niggers. You can put fancy clothes on them, but they is still niggers. You can tell by the smell. Show me your papers, boy!"

Simon stepped in and said, "Sir, Josiah is a freeman in my employ as my man servant. If you must see his papers, I will show them to you."

"I do require this, sir. He might be one of them runaways that we are hunting." Then, looking at Josiah, he continued, "Where are you gentlemen headin?" He said this mockingly, indicating that he probably didn't think Josiah merited being called a gentleman.

Simon started to answer, but the slave hunter held up his hand and said, "I want to hear this from the nigger's mouth."

Josiah swallowed nervously and said, "Sir, our destination is Morgantown, Virginia. My employer, the Reverend Mr. Albrecht, has been called to pastor a church in that town." Josiah said this with the proper diction and grammar that Simon had taught him on their journey thus far.

The slave hunter was surprised, "Well said. But I know that you are just aping your masters 'cause even a house nigger don't normally learn to talk like that."

Simon handed the slave hunter Josiah's certificate of status as a free man. The slave hunter took it in his hand and made a show of reading it. Then, pointing at Simon, he said, "So, you are a reverend, huh? Well, I guess everything is in order, so we'll let you go on your way. But know this: if we find out your nigger heah is a runaway, we'll hunt you down in Morgantown and bring both of y'all to justice!"

"Understood, sir! We will be resuming our journey now, and we wish you all the best the Lord can give!" Then in his thoughts, and I hope that means long sentences in prison.

The slave hunters moved aside and watched the buckboard wagon continue on its northwesterly path. When they were out of earshot, the leader grunted and said, "Somethin weren't right about that preacher man and his freed manservant. Let's be looking for their description on the runaway slave notices when we get a chance."

CHAPTER FOUR

"Mr. Simon, do you think we've seen the last of them?"

"I don't know for sure, but their leader didn't appear to be convinced. Keep in mind that some of these slave hunters will capture freemen and take them down south to be sold as slaves. No, I don't trust these characters. We need to be on the lookout for patrols like this."

"If your father notices your absence, he might think you have escaped the plantation, and alert the slave catchers. But that won't happen until sometime Monday. What I don't know is how quickly the posters are printed and distributed. We might have two or three days at most before we encounter slave hunters looking for you."

"I'm sorry to have called all this evil down on you, Mister Simon. It's me they be after, not you!"

"Josiah, there will always be evil in the world, but remember as Christians we have the Holy Spirit standing beside us, an ever-present help in times of trouble. Evil men can kill our physical bodies, but they can't kill our eternal spirits."

"Well, I get that, sir. I just don't want to leave this physical body anytime soon!"

"Morgantown is 167 miles from Middleburg. We are finishing our first full day of travel and I figure we have gone about 35 miles. At this rate we should reach Morgantown in four or five days, and then travel another seven or so miles to cross the state line to Pennsylvania.

In the great state of Pennsylvania, the first state to declare slavery illegal, Josiah, you will be a free man!"

Smiling broadly and clapping his hands, Josiah said, "That be music to mah ears!"

As the sun began to set, they drove the wagon into a break in a grove of trees. They didn't bother with the tent because there had been no threat of rain. A shallow stream ran nearby, so they had water for the mules and water to make the cornmeal biscuits they would have for dinner and breakfast. A simple meal but well-appreciated at the end of a long day. They also boiled some coffee and sipped from their cups as they watched the campfire. As they began to feel a bit drowsy, Simon lit a kerosene lamp and read some of the Bible aloud for Josiah's benefit.

"Before we fall asleep, I just want to remind you of the promises we have from God Himself. In Romans, Chapter 8, St. Paul said, 'If God is for us, who can be against us?' Psalm 46 tells us that God is our refuge and strength, a very present help in trouble. And Psalm 138 says 'Though I walk in the midst of trouble, you preserve my life; you stretch out your hand against the wrath of my enemies, and your right hand delivers me.'"

"I'll be countin on them promises, Mr. Simon; and when my reading is ready for it, the Bible will be the first book I read. Good night, sir!"

Five uneventful days passed, with Simon tutoring Josiah on his reading, grammar, and diction. The travelers then encountered the Monongahela River, which they had to cross to continue across the state line into Pennsylvania. There wasn't a bridge nearby, but when asking a local person on the street about a ferry, they were pointed in the right direction for a ferry they could take.

"There's a horse ferry (some people call it a team ferry) about two miles upriver. Your mules will join the other mules or horses and walk in circles to power the paddle wheels. It's a slow means of locomotion, but it does the job! Are your mules in good shape, fellows?"

"I think Ruth and Naomi will do all right. Of course, they've never been on a boat before, so I don't know if they will find that frightening!" said Simon.

"If'n they just concentrate on the horse's ass in front of them, they will do fine."

The ferry boat was exactly where the local man said it would be. The ferryman instructed the young men on where to position their mules, joining two horses already harnessed and ready to go. Ruth and Naomi caught on quickly to their new task, and the ferry boat ride across the river was uneventful.

Josiah was ecstatic with his newfound freedom; his spirit was buoyed, and it seemed that nothing could stop him from attaining his dream of a new life in Canada. Then, suddenly, everything changed.

The three slave hunters had arrived in Morgantown and were checking the latest notices for runaway slaves at the sheriff's office. They had failed in their pursuit of Samson and Esther, the couple they had described to Simon and Josiah, and now were hoping to get leads on other runaway slaves. They were in luck because Henry Lee Howell's notice for a runaway slave had been telegraphed to the Morgantown sheriff. It read as follows:

Missing from the home of Colonel Henry Lee Howell of Middleburg, Virginia, a light-skinned male Negro named Josiah. He is about 18 years of age and stands about six feet tall. He might be traveling with a young white man, Simon Albrecht, who is an abolitionist preacher. The monetary reward for the return of this male slave in a sound body and in good health will exceed his value on the auction block.

The leader of this particular group of slave hunters went by the name of Captain Jude Lawless, the military rank being something he was awarded when he volunteered his men, Franklin and Samuel, and himself to the Virginia state militia. Soon, he figured the lucrative business of catching runaways and returning them to their masters or selling them to a slaver would be drawing to a close as plantation owners, still young enough to accept commissions in the Confederate Army, left their plantations to serve in the glorious defense of their commonwealth against Northern aggressors.

When the "captain" found the description of Josiah, he slapped his thigh and said,

"Boys, Ah knew something wasn't right about that uppity pale nigger we met headed north a few days ago. He lied to us about bein free. Those liars weren't stoppin in Morgantown, they was gonna cross the state line into Pennsylvania, where that darkie would become a free man! Let's ride hard to catch up with them and fetch his black ass back to Virginia to his rightful master. We'll pursue them far into Pennsylvania and even into Canada if we must! This reward will be mighty handsome, count on it!"

Two men riding horses happened to converge on the road headed east in West Central Pennsylvania. As they drew closer, they realized they were both Indians, which by this point in history was unusual in

the eastern United States, with most Indian nations removed to reservations. The two riders raised their hands in a friendly greeting and began conversing as they rode along.

"Good day, sir! I am Blue Feather Chouteau of Missouri, and who might you be?"

"Good day, Blue Feather! I am Ely Parker from New York. I am a member of the Seneca Nation."

"Ah, you are the first Seneca I've met! My mother's family is of the Osage Nation. I have not spent much time in the East."

"And your father's family? French descent, I'd guess."

"Good guess."

"Oh, come to think of it – I think Sam Grant (that is, Ulysses S. Grant) mentioned you! I met him in Galena, Illinois."

"Yes, Sam Grant recruited me as a scout and interpreter for the U.S. Army. I served for a time in Texas and then in the northwest and California. How is Sam Grant these days?"

"I'm sorry to say that Sam has run into some hard times. When I met him, he was working as a clerk in his father's leather goods store. He had run afoul of his superiors in the Army for alleged drunkenness. After being drummed out of the Army, he tried farming in Missouri with little success, and then moved back to Galena where I was serving as an engineer overseeing government projects such as the construction of a custom house and marine hospital. I had a similar job in Dubuque, Iowa. Most recently I've been in charge of lighthouse construction on the Great Lakes."

"I want to dispel the notion that Sam Grant is a drunk! It's just that he reacts adversely to alcohol. Even a small drink can affect him."

"Well, I can believe that! He is a man of good character. I understand that he is now trying to get reinstated with the Army but having some difficulties."

"Then I will pray for him, because the nation needs men like him now."

"I am headed back to New York where I hope to establish a regiment of Indian soldiers to fight for the Union. I heard some interesting things about you, Blue Feather. For example, that before you served as a scout and interpreter for the Army, you served as a translator for the famous Fr. DeSmet on his missions to the western Indian tribes. You must know a variety of Indian languages."

"That's true, and it's interesting to see a white person's expression when they learn just how many languages and cultures there are among the Indians of North America."

"So, why are you traveling east?"

"I've been invited to discuss Indian beliefs and cultures with a scholar named Lewis Henry Morgan."

"Wow! It's a small world – I met Professor Morgan some years ago when he was studying the Iroquois people. He published his work in 1851 in a book titled League of the Iroquois.

"Yes, I read this book and discussed it with Fr. De Smet!"

"If I recall correctly, you are a scholar and a graduate of St. Louis College."

"Yes, that is true – at least the part about being a graduate of St. Louis College. I am guessing that you must be a college man yourself."

"I am indeed. I studied engineering at Rensselaer Polytechnic Institute."

Finding common interests, the men decided to travel together until their destinations required them to take different directions.

Blue Feather spotted the trouble first, "Ely, look ahead! It seems that someone has been accosted by highwaymen."

He was referring to Simon Albrecht, now alone, who was struggling to stand up. He held his head where he had been bludgeoned, probably pistol-whipped. Ely and Blue Feather loped over to Simon.

"What happened here? Was it highwaymen? It looks like you will have quite a knot on your noggin, if not a concussion," said Ely.

Simon was dazed and trying to steady himself by holding onto a wagon wheel.

"Where is Josiah? Oh, geez – they took Josiah!"

"Who took Josiah? Is Josiah your son?"

"Josiah is a former slave, a young man of 18 years. We were moving to Canada for a fresh start. I am a seminary graduate hoping to be called to the pastorate. Josiah is hoping for an apprenticeship under a skilled tradesman. The hoodlums who mugged me and kidnapped Josiah are slave hunters."

"How many of them were there?"

"Just three, rough-looking and armed thugs."

"When were you attacked?

Simon took a quick look at his pocket watch, "It was about thirty minutes ago. We might still catch them if we ride hard."

Looking at Ely for affirmation, Blue Feather said, "Simon, we'll overtake these hoodlums and try to rescue Josiah from their clutches. I assume that they were headed south for Virginia, where your friend could be sold as a slave or returned to his master. But you are not in any shape to go with us. We need to get you to a place where you can rest and recover. I'll bet a Quaker family will provide help and shelter to an abolitionist preacher, or so I am guessing, who has been injured."

Simon protested, but Ely and Blue Feather unfurled his bedroll and laid it out for him in the bed of the wagon. Simon said to Ely, "Do you have a weapon? If not, please take my Colt, which I have in a shoulder holster."

"I guess your attackers didn't expect a young minister to be toting a revolver, and they didn't pat you down."

"Well, I got clunked on the head so hard I fell off the wagon and did not have the presence of mind or the wherewithal to fire it!"

They stopped at the first farmhouse they saw, which belonged to a Quaker family.

A tall man in his fifties dressed in black watched as they pulled into the farmyard. He walked right up to Blue Feather, who was driving the wagon.

"Good day sirs! How might we help thee?"

"We have a young minister of the Word lying in the bed of this wagon. He was transporting a young free colored man named Josiah to a new life in Canada when a band of slave hunters attacked them. They bludgeoned Simon, the man you see lying here, and kidnapped the colored man. If we might leave Simon in your hands for a few days so that he might recover, my friend and I will pursue the kidnappers and rescue Josiah."

"We would be pleased to serve the Lord in this manner," said the farmer, whose name was Joseph Rowntree. Joseph and his wife Elizabeth had five daughters and no sons. This would present a challenge to Simon later, with the girls vying for his attention.

Blue Feather and Ely galloped south in search of the slave hunters. They figured the slave hunters had a two-hour head start on them, but also figured they would not be in a hurry and might trot along at about four miles per hour. If they could pursue the slave hunters at a twelve-mile-per-hour pace for an hour, they might catch up to them.

And so, it happened an hour or so later, they could see the slavers ahead of them a short distance.

Ely drew close to Blue Feather and asked, "Do you have a plan?"

"Yes, let's nonchalantly flank them and then quickly draw our weapons. We will get the drop on them and force them to throw down their weapons. While I keep a gun on them, you dismount and pick up their guns, empty them and heave them into that pond on the right."

The plan was executed almost perfectly. What they didn't account for was the two-shot derringer the captain held in his jacket! He was aiming at Blue Feather and ready to fire when a rock the size of a baseball hit him on the head, causing him to fall from his horse. The derringer had fallen about three feet from his hand, and Blue Feather quickly picked it up.

"Who threw that rock? Whoever you are, you probably saved my life!"

A very large man came forward and said, "I did, Samson Culpeper." The man speaking was a very dark Negro slave, standing about six feet, three inches tall, and weighing about 270 pounds. He and his wife, Esther, had been hiding in a grove of trees. They slept during the day and traveled at night. They had successfully evaded the slave hunters for hundreds of miles from North Carolina to this point in Pennsylvania.

"These crackers been huntin us for weeks now. Ah saw what was happenin, and Ah decided to help free dis here young man from they clutches. It's about time they taste some of they own medicine. Let's tie them up deep in this grove of trees, and maybe gag them with they own shirts."

Ely pulled out Josiah's gag, and Josiah said, "Let me help you with that Samson!"

"Splendid idea! I happen to have plenty of rope with me!" said Blue Feather.

Fifteen minutes later, after the three slave hunters were gagged and tied to trees deep in the grove, Ely and Blue Feather explained who they were to Josiah, "We ran across your friend Simon, and brought him to a nearby farm where he could recover from his injuries. He told us what had happened, and we decided to rescue you. We'll take you to him now. Samson, the slave hunters have graciously donated their horses so that you and your lady can continue your journey on horseback!"

"Dis is mighty kind of y'all!" said Samson. "But you two must be Injuns – I never in mah life would expect help from a white man and I didn't expect otherwise from Injuns."

"You should know there are people of every color who want to do whatever is good and righteous, Samson," said Blue Feather. "You and your missus are free now to start a new life."

"Samson, I want to thank you for helpin rescue me. Now I'm goin to resume my trek to Canada, where slavery has been outlawed, and there are some towns where Black people have congregated and built good lives for themselves. Chatham is where I am goin," said Josiah.

Samson smiled and said, "Dat be where me and the missus be headed! We'll see you there!"

CHAPTER FIVE

Some days before Josiah's abduction by the slave hunters, a group of runaway slaves arrived at the farm of Joseph Rowntree, a stationmaster for the Underground Railroad. There were fifteen persons in this group led by a "conductor" named Alphonse. This particular group had started in New Orleans and had been joined by other escapees as it worked its way through Louisiana, Arkansas, Tennessee, Kentucky, and Ohio. One member of this group had twisted her ankle and was slowing down progress. Alphonse wanted to discuss this matter with the stationmaster, Joseph Rowntree, when the fugitives appeared at Joseph's barn around 5:00 in the morning.

"Mr. Rowntree, we have a member of our group, a young woman, who cannot continue with us because she has injured her ankle. She is slowing us down and this puts us at risk of being caught."

"Do you mean sir, the white girl I saw limping in the barn with her ankle wrapped? What is a white girl doing with your group?"

"Yes, that is the girl! But she isn't white according to Louisiana law. She has one black great-grandparent, so she is one-eighth black and that is enough to classify her as black and to justify keeping her as a slave."

Mrs. Rowntree joined them at this moment and heard Alphonse say that the girl was black in the eyes of the law.

"Husband, the girl should stay with us, at least until she is able to travel again. I will dress her in the plain clothes we wear in the Society of Friends, and no one will know the difference!

"Yes, and we will treat her just like her sisters! Alphonse, my wife and I will speak with her now. Oh, but what is her name?"

"Her name is Gabrielle Marie. I don't know if she has a last name."

Gabrielle was easy to locate. The Rowntrees went to her, rather than ask her to hobble over.

Elizabeth Rowntree spoke for them, "Gabrielle, we just now spoke with Alphonse. Thou are welcome to stay with us until your ankle heals or as long as you like. Thou will be treated like one of our daughters and stay in our house as one of the family. And thou should address us as Mother and Father. Does this appeal to thee?"

Gabrielle was taken aback by this offer. She had never had a normal family experience and had longed for one. It took her some seconds to mull over the offer because although she wanted a family, she was initially reluctant to commit herself. But after a brief delay, she said, "Why, yes, Mother and Father! I would be honored to join your family, if only for a season!"

"We belong to the Society of Friends or Quakers, which thou might not have encountered before. We have a simple form of the Christian faith. We believe that if we do the work of Christ, we shall come to know who he is. We can discuss this more at a later time, but for now, simply know this – that we try to live in accordance with what we call the Inner Light, and others might call the Holy Spirit. Everything we think, say, or do must be consistent with God's will and honor Him."

"Father will bring out a pair of crutches for thee, and then I will take thee to our bathhouse where thou can wash with soap and clean water. I will bring thee some clean clothes in the plain Quaker style."

Gabrielle felt wonderful to be clean again after weeks on the road without a proper bath. As she was drying herself afterwards, Elizabeth returned with fresh clothes. The dress and bonnet were navy blue cotton, plain and functional, and so attired Gabrielle could easily be perceived as the sixth daughter in the family.

"Oh, now daughter, thou looks just like one of the family!" exclaimed Elizabeth.

"Mother, I have something that I must tell you, especially since I am being welcomed into this pious family," said Gabrielle, with tears forming in her eyes.

"Gabrielle, whatever is troubling thee, can be shared with me without judgment."

"In New Orleans and then in Lexington, Kentucky I was a "fancy girl." I was a slave kept at a bordello with ten other girls, all octoroons or quadroons. We were hired out to prominent white gentlemen in the city for their sexual gratification. Evenings would start with a ball in the bordello's ballroom. The gentlemen guests paid the admission price, and then they could dance with the girls. The fancy girls were taught how to talk to a gentleman and how to read poetry to them. Some were taught the piano or how to sing. So, we appeared be young women of sophisticated upbringing. As the evening came to a close, the gentlemen would choose a girl for sexual purposes. Mother, I had been forced into this life when I was sixteen by my own father, a white plantation owner. I was never paid for my services. My father and the bordello owners shared whatever I earned."

"I had begged my father not to use me in this manner, but he showed no mercy. My mother was a quadroon who had served in the same capacity. My father purchased her from the bordello when she became pregnant by him. She died when I was twelve years old, and she never knew about my father's plan for me."

Tears were streaming down both women's faces, with Gabrielle sobbing as Elizabeth held her.

"Child, God knows that thou hast not sinned, and He has brought thee to this family to be healed and to be brought closer to Him. Thou hast thy whole life before thee, and I have faith that thou wilt be blessed abundantly. Thy secret is safe with me – I shall be the sole keeper of thy secret."

Gabrielle sobbed out a thank you and wiped her tears with the bath towel. She then resolved in her mind that she would pray for this experience of the Inner Light.

Elizabeth led Gabrielle to the bedroom, which she would share with Faith, the eldest daughter, who was not bothered about sharing her previously private room. Afterwards Gabrielle met her new sisters Faith, Hope, Charity, Mercy, and Joy. Faith and Gabrielle were both 20 years of age. After Faith, new sisters were added every two years.

The Rowntree girls were peppering their new sister with questions.

Faith asked, "Gabrielle, how was it that you were traveling with runaway slaves?"

"It's because that is what I am! I am a runaway slave!"

"But you are as white as we are!" exclaimed Joy.

"Louisiana law says that a person like me, who has just one black great-grandparent, is black and unless her parents are free persons, she must serve as a slave. My mother had one black grandparent and she was a slave."

"So, the plantation owner didn't put you out in the field to do heavy farm labor in the sun? You are a blonde with fair skin. You would have burned up!"

"No, I was hired out to a type of hotel... Well, I don't want to go into details. Let's just say that I wanted out of that establishment. Dear sisters, I want to swear you all to secrecy – no one outside of this family must know I am an escaped slave. If the slave hunters ever caught wind of who I am I could be captured and brought back to my former master or sold as a slave to a new master."

The oldest sister, Faith, then looked sternly around the room at her sisters and said, "Gabrielle, do not worry we will not breathe word of this to anyone! Your secret is safe with us."

Then, after a moment of embarrassed silence, Faith said, "Oh my, look at your shoes! They appear to be all worn out from your long walk. We'll have to do something about that. You need proper footwear. We will have to get you some new shoes."

The next day, the girls became aware of two new visitors to the farm, Simon and Josiah, who were sleeping in the barn in the hidden rooms for the escaped slaves, i.e., passengers on the underground railroad. Simon was injured with a concussion, bruised ribs, and some cuts and bruises on his face because after being knocked cold with the butt of a pistol, he had fallen first on the wagon wheel and then on the gravel road and so required some nursing. Elizabeth assigned Simon's care and feeding to Gabrielle since the other girls already had regular responsibilities. Josiah volunteered to help with the farm's horses and mules and whatever physical tasks Mr. Rowntree might have on the farm.

Gabrielle introduced herself to Simon and Josiah on the afternoon of the second day of their stay on the farm.

"Good afternoon, gentlemen! My name is Gabrielle and Mother has asked me to help take care of you during your recovery."

Simon said, "That will be very kind of you!" My name is Simon Albrecht, and my friend here is Josiah DeMornay."

"Where were you gentlemen headed when you were attacked by the highwaymen?"

Josiah answered for them, "We were headed for Chatham, Canada. But they weren't highwaymen. They were slave hunters bound and determined to capture me and return me to my master in Virginia."

"Josiah was posing as my free manservant. We thought that this ruse might discourage slave hunters from bothering us. But Josiah's alleged status as a freeman didn't deter the slave hunters from physical violence in abducting him."

"After they knocked out Simon with a pistol-whipping, they ganged up on me and bound and gagged me."

"Two Indian men, civilized fellows, saw me on the road trying to stand and brought me here and then tracked down the slave hunters and freed Josiah."

"Oh, my goodness! Well, thank God for your rescuers! They were like the good Samaritan in the Bible."

"Yes, my thoughts exactly! Have you read much of the Bible?" asked Simon.

"Yes, besides the McGuffy Reader, the Farmer's Almanac, and some collections of poetry, it was the only book we had in the household."

"Mr. Simon has been teaching me to read, but I am not very good at it yet. Once we get to Canada, I hope to be a good reader and find myself a job."

"So, Canada is your destination. There you will be free no matter where you go. And Simon, were you planning to move to Canada?"

"Yes, if I had stayed in Virginia, I would be expected to join the Confederate army and defend the practice of slavery and help undo the great American experiment of government by the people. I can't do that in good conscience. And I can't join the Union army either, because that would mean fighting against people who were my friends and neighbors."

"So, you are hoping to flee to a neutral country. I can understand that."

"Yes, neutral but more than that. Over many years, Black people who had escaped from their masters and followed the underground railroad to its terminus in Chatham, Canada have established towns in which former slaves can thrive. I want to help people in these towns succeed if I can. Their success should be a great testimony against slavery in the United States."

Gabrielle smiled at the young blonde man and his sense of righteousness. She started to feel some affection for him, which surprised her some because her usual reaction to men was resentment and even revulsion because she felt used by them.

For his part, Simon was instantly attracted to this beautiful young woman with dark blonde hair who tenderly washed the cuts and scrapes on his face. He felt a strong physical attraction despite his headache and bruised ribs.

Gabrielle finished her gentle washing of Simon's face and said, "Josiah, could you help Simon to the bathhouse and fill the bathtub for him? There are towels and soap there. You can take the chill off the water by adding hot water. You will find a pump, bucket, and a fireplace there for this purpose."

Josiah quickly assumed the role of servant again, eager to please the master's pretty daughter, saying, "Yes, Miss Gabrielle. I'll get right on that. I'll run over now and get the tub filled, then I'll come back for you, Massa Simon."

"Josiah, you don't need to put 'master' in front of 'Simon'!"

"Whatever you say, sir!"

Gabrielle caught the slight exasperation on Simon's face and briefly smiled. She thought, He's trying his best to encourage Josiah out of his slave mindset!

Josiah returned after drawing the bath to help Simon to the bathhouse. As Simon eased himself into the tub, Josiah snickered and said, "You must be thinking of Miss Gabrielle!"

"Josiah, grant me some privacy, please!"

"Yes, sir!"

Gabrielle knocked on the door to the bathhouse and said, "I'm setting down some clean clothes I found in your carpet bag. When you've dried yourself and have your pants on, please allow me to enter. I want to wrap your ribs like the doctor would."

Josiah opened his eyes wide, smiled at Simon, and whispered, "Now that is what I call service!"

Simon snapped his wet towel at Josiah, who quickly jumped out of the way, and he immediately regretted it for the pain it caused to his ribs, "Ouch, I should not have done that!"

Josiah went to the door to allow Gabrielle access. "Mother gave me this linen sheet to cut into a long strip for wrapping your ribs. Please sit here on the bench so that I can wrap this tightly around your chest."

Gabrielle noticed that Simon was well-built for a bookish sort of young man, and then, realizing where her thoughts were going, quickly averted her gaze. But Josiah noticed her reaction and filed it away.

As Josiah helped Gabrielle wrap Simon's rib cage, Simon looked down and saw the sorry state of Gabrielle's shoes. "Gabrielle, you need a new pair of shoes! I might be able to help you with that."

"Oh, how so?"

Josiah quickly answered, "Mister Simon has more than his book learning, which is considerable. He also knows how to make shoes! These shoes I'm wearin were made by Mr. Simon."

"Goodness, those look like well-made shoes, very sturdy!"

"If you bring me an example of a Quaker lady's shoe, I'll start to work tomorrow on a new pair."

"But you will need some leather would you not?"

"I have some leather left over from Josiah's pair. I used only a half a cow to make his shoes!" said Simon with a twinkle in his eye.

Josiah laughed, "OK, truth be told, I do have big feet. My mama used to say that no hurricane would ever blow me over!"

Gabrielle could not help but laugh, and it was the first laugh she had had in a very long time. "Thank you for making me laugh! Simon, I will bring one of my sister's shoes as a model."

"She can be wearing it, of course. And I will need some paper and a pencil to trace out your foot."

Just before the evening meal, Gabrielle brought Faith with her to Simon's quarters. "Hello, Simon, Faith and I are here to have my foot measured for a new pair of shoes!"

Faith's four younger sisters tagged along because they wanted to see the "handsome young man" their sister Faith had described to them.

Simon looked up from his Bible, stood up carefully, and smiled. "It's good to see you again, Gabrielle, and to meet you, Faith. And who are these other young ladies?"

"Oh, these are my younger sisters, Hope, Charity, Mercy, and Joy." The girls were all smiling and blushing. Then the youngest sister, Joy, said, "Mother said I should not be considering marriage just yet because I am just twelve years old. This should help you narrow down your choice some."

This revelation elicited a chorus of groans from her sisters. Hope then said, "OK, sisters, it's time for you to start the supper preparation." Then, she practically pushed them out of the room.

Simon just laughed quietly but then pressed his ribs. "Ouch, I guess I'm not recovered enough for laughter!"

Simon looked at Gabrielle's stockinged foot and held it a bit longer than necessary, "Well, what a well-proportioned foot you have!"

Faith stifled a snicker and caught Gabrielle's eye. Gabrielle just looked embarrassed. Simon then took his measurements and consulted a sizing chart. Finally, he announced, "You are a size 6 with a medium width."

Faith sat down and took off her shoe for Simon to examine. He quickly made a few sketches and asked, "Is this shoe typical of the style Quaker women wear? I can make it a bit fancier if you like."

"Oh no, please keep it plain. I want to fit in."

As they walked back to the house, Faith smiled and looked at Gabrielle.

"What are you smiling about, dear sister?"

"It's just how that young man's whole countenance brightened when you stepped into the room! He is quite taken with you!"

Blushing, Gabrielle said, "Really, oh shush!"

"I can see that you like him as well!"

"Like I said, "Shush!"

CHAPTER SIX

It took Simon three days to make the shoes. This was a labor of about ten hours, but because of his injuries, he could work only about three hours per day. Gabrielle tried on the shoes, and they fit perfectly. Simon was pleased to be able to give Gabrielle these shoes and see her happy. But then he felt his happiness was bound to end. Like the Bible says, there is a season for everything.

Mrs. Rowntree came to visit Simon soon after Gabrielle received her new shoes with a proposition. "Simon, thou are going to need another four weeks or more before thou are mended well enough to continue thy long journey to Canada. Mr. Rowntree and I have discussed the situation, and we would like thee and Josiah to stay with us until thou feel well enough to travel. In the meantime, it would be an immense help to this family if thee would teach our girls about the Bible, history, English composition, and mathematics and other subjects thou are prepared to teach. We would greatly appreciate it! Does this seem to thee a fair proposition?"

"It seems to me quite fair, and I would be pleased to serve your family in this manner! And I suppose Josiah could continue to assist Mr. Rowntree with various farm tasks?"

"Yes, Josiah has proven most helpful, and he is especially handy with the horses and mules. Josiah should be welcome to attend the school when he is not needed with a farm task. We had heard that thou have been helping Josiah with his book learning on your journey, and we would not want to interfere with that!"

"Oh, but what about books from which I could develop my lessons? And a blackboard and chalk, and slates for the students?"

"We already have slates and a blackboard. And we have not yet shown thee Mr. Rowntree's personal library, but in it thou will find many books on history, English grammar and composition, as well as the Bible. Thou will be well-equipped to develop thy lessons!"

"What will we use as a classroom?"

"Well, thou will hold open-air classes until Mr. Rowntree and Josiah can build the meeting house."

"A meeting house?"

"Yes, the Society of Friends holds meetings (thou would call them services) on Sunday mornings, and we will build the first meeting place for Quakers in this neighborhood."

"What is a Quaker service like? I'm guessing it is nothing like the liturgical service we have in the Lutheran Church."

"No, it is quite different. Friends gather in silence in the presence of God. In silence, we may worship and listen to the voice of the Spirit. Out of the silence, messages from God may also come to us in the spoken word or prayer. Thus, a member might stand and share a prophecy, or a prayer. Another might stand and deliver a short sermon, if he feels the message is coming from God."

"I see what you mean about being different. I'm sure that it is acceptable to God to be worshipped in that manner. This is the only thing that matters.

The Rowntree girls decided to call Simon 'Professor' because it seemed to them that his knowledge went far beyond what the typical teacher could bring to the classroom. The school was a great success because the girls really enjoyed the opportunity to learn, and Simon put a great deal of effort into his teaching. Gabrielle especially appreciated the experience because formal schooling was entirely new to her. Oftentimes, she would linger after class to ask questions or to debate a point made in the lesson. Both Simon and Gabrielle looked forward to this time together, and on several occasions, they would continue their discussions as they strolled the perimeter of the farm. Simon was impressed by her insights into issues and told her so. She appreciated his compliments because previously, men had only praised her for her beauty, and their intentions were clear. Gabrielle felt both comfortable with and attracted to Simon, and as her attraction grew deeper, she began to dread the day they would have to part company. And her thoughts always turned to Simon's fiancé back home in Virginia. Does he still yearn for her and want to marry her?

The construction of the meeting house was delayed by at least two weeks, but once other Quaker men in the neighborhood heard of Mr. Rowntree's plan, they organized a "barn-raising" party, much like the practice of their in-state neighbors, the Amish. Thus, Simon and Josiah ended up staying five weeks rather than the original two weeks. For the last four weeks, Simon held his classes in the new meeting house.

On one of their walks, Gabrielle gently questioned Simon about his plans for the future.

"Simon, do you think you will make Canada your permanent residence, or will you return to the U.S. after the war has concluded?"

"To be honest, I think that depends on the outcome of the war and what Emily wants to do. If the Union wins the war, the south will likely be devastated and require a period of reconstruction. Plantations and farms will likely need a lot of work before they can become productive again. And people will need time to adjust to a new economic and social order once the slaves become free men. I don't think plantation owners like Emily's father will like the changes they will inevitably face. Emily might want to stay close to her mother to help her through the transition, which I suspect will strain the relationship between Emily's parents. If the Confederates win the war (which I think is unlikely), there still will be a lot of work to be done before the plantations and farms can become productive again. Come to think of it, Emily might want to stay close to her parents, to help them through the rebuilding of their plantation, win or lose."

"You know, Simon, when you return to Virginia after the war people might think of you as someone who ran away to Canada to avoid the trials and tribulations that people loyal to Virginia had to live through. You might meet with a lot of resentment. Forgive me for saying this, but do you think your died-in-the-wool Confederate father-in-law would ever welcome you into the family?"

"Gabrielle, honestly, no – I never will be good enough for Emily in her father's eyes, if only because I told him I thought slavery was immoral. He no doubt took my opposition to slavery as a rejection of his way of life and everything he holds dear. I have come to think that if Emily and I do indeed get married, we will have to live apart from her parents, perhaps even in the North. And Emily will have to learn how to live without her accustomed wealth and privilege. When we last spoke, Emily was thinking she might lose her inheritance if she married me against her father's will."

"Oh, dear Simon – do you really love this girl? And does she really love you, enough to endure these hardships of a disapproving father, loss of wealth, and estrangement from her family?"

Simon looked away for some seconds and then down at his shoes. "I honestly don't know what I feel anymore, but as a Southern gentleman, I feel honor-bound to try to be true to my promise to her.

Her love for me might not be strong enough for these new circumstances that the war has presented. I don't know what to feel or what to think! If she still wants to marry me with all these potential conditions, I would be surprised."

"You asked me if I still loved her. The answer is yes, but it is not a burning, passionate love. Instead, it is the kind of love that develops between a boy and a girl who practically grew up together. Perhaps that is not the right kind of love to build a marriage on, I don't know."

"Simon, I've heard that a lot of marriages are not based on romantic love – that is something that develops later. But I personally would not want that kind of marriage. I would prefer to think that God has brought me to the man I should love and marry. But maybe I am simply a dreamer!"

"And I'm probably a dreamer to think that a marriage to Emily would ever work out well…" Simon's voice trailing off.

A few days later, it appeared that this chapter of Simon's life was coming to a close.

"Gabrielle, it's about time for Josiah and me to resume our journey to Canada. I must tell you I don't want to leave the Rowntrees' farm just yet. I want to spend more time with you and your family (Simon, being careful not to be overly specific). But your family probably doesn't feel the same way," his voice trailing.

"Oh, I think everyone in this family would be pleased to have you and Josiah stay on indefinitely. But you have a mission to fulfill with Josiah, don't you? I thought that you were moving to Canada to help him start a new life, helping him to learn a trade, and to read and write so that he can function as an independent free man. When you set out on this mission you thought that the best place for this new life would be in Canada in a distinctly black town. He would have his best chances of success in such a town."

"Yes, I believe that all to be true still."

"Simon, why don't you make a point of visiting us here in Pennsylvania for Christmas and Easter? And please write me when you get settled in Canada. I don't want us to drift apart."

The morning of their departure, the Rowntree family prepared them a big breakfast. Afterwards, Josiah harnessed the mules, Ruth and Naomi, attached them to the buckboard wagon, and drove it to the center of the barnyard where everyone was gathering. Mr. Rowntree walked up to Simon carrying a box. Handing it to Simon, he said, "Your rescuers, the two Indian fellows, said that this weapon belongs to you. Apparently, they used this in their effort to rescue Josiah from the slave hunters. As Quakers, we do not arm ourselves or fight in wars, but I can understand why you would want a revolver on your journey for self-defense."

"Thank you, Mr. Rowntree, for keeping this in a secure spot for us. I sincerely hope and pray I never have to use it because I abhor violence."

Pointing at the wagon bed, Josiah said, "I loaded up all our belongings – the carpet bags, the shoemaking tools, your Bible and the Bible commentaries, bedrolls, the tent, canteens and cookware. But look what Mr. Rowntree is giving us – a waterproof canvas to cover our belongings!

"Thank you very much, Mr. Rowntree! And thank you, Mrs. Rowntree for the loaves of bread and jars of apple butter!

Shyly, Gabrielle came forward and hugged Simon, whispering in his ear, "Please write me and tell me what you experience in Canada. I will respond to each letter!"

Josiah drove the wagon out of the Rowntree property and continued northward to Canada.

"Well, you surely charmed that Miss Gabrielle all lickety-split! From the beginning that girl was taken with you! I could see it in her eyes when she was taking care of you, and I'll tell you what really clinched it for me was the way she looked at you with your shirt off. Dang brother, I had never figured you as a ladies' man!"

"OK, enough already about Miss Gabrielle! You are embarrassing me, and I know Miss Gabrielle would not want you to be carrying on like this!"

"Sorry, Mr. Simon! I'll keep my observations to mahself. But man, where did you get all them muscles? It wasn't from hard work; I know that to be true!"

Simon ignored the playful dig and said, "I guess it's from my time on the boxing team at Gettysburg and before that, my membership with the turnverein (that's German for gymnastics club)."

"But we didn't have a gymnastics club in Middleburg, did we?"

"No, we didn't. Before I knew you, I spent a few summers with relatives in Baltimore where they were members of the Turner Hall. It was more than a gymnasium – it also served as a center for social and political events."

"So, that means you are strong and know how to fight!"

"Well, knowing how to box according to the collegiate rules might not be that useful against a knife-wielding ruffian. For the rules to work, both sides need to abide by them."

"I suppose that means you gotta take that knockout punch early in the fight!"

"Well, let's just pray I don't find myself in such a predicament!"

Hours passed in their trek northward, and Josiah spotted two riders trotting toward them. Josiah passed the field glasses to Simon and said, "Look ahead, Mr. Simon. We might have some company in a few minutes. Nothing to worry about, I hope."

"Well, I'm pretty sure these fellows are not slave catchers – they appear to be too neatly dressed for that. Oh, but they are wearing Union uniforms! Try your best not to sound too Southern in your speech. Be mindful of your diction."

Moments later, the two riders stopped in their tracks, and one rider put up his hand to indicate that Josiah and Simon should pull over to the side of the road. The riders were a colonel and a sergeant major. The colonel greeted them, "Good afternoon, gentleman. I am Colonel Wilson, and my companion here is Sergeant Major Harrison. We are on a recruiting drive for a new volunteer regiment for western Pennsylvania. Where might you be from?"

"I am Simon Albrecht, and my friend here is Josiah De Mornay. We are from Gettysburg traveling northwest to Sandusky, Ohio."

"Mr. Albrecht, is it? Son, you don't sound like you are from Pennsylvania. I'm detecting something vaguely southern in your accent. Gentlemen, the sergeant major and I need to search your cargo. Sergeant Major, please proceed."

The sergeant major rather sloppily searched through their belongings, tossing items left and right, digging out the contents of their carpet bags, and dispersing them haphazardly. This continued until the sergeant major exclaimed, "Ho boy, what do we have here?"

He handed a hard-covered notebook to the colonel and said, "Colonel, this here is a blank notebook, and look where it was printed – Atlanta, Georgia!"

"Now that is very interesting indeed! What exactly were you going to write on these blank pages, Mr. Albrecht? Observations of troop strength, location, and readiness to send back to your Confederate friends? You do realize that if you are a Confederate soldier traveling out of uniform, you can be arrested as a spy and then be shot by a firing squad?"

Shaking his head, the colonel said, "Boys, I must ask you to step down and place your hands on the wagon. We need to search your persons."

"Colonel, I must object! We have done nothing wrong! We are headed to Sandusky, where I will be pastoring a Lutheran church."

Patting down Simon, the Colonel discovered his revolver. "Well, now, how many pastors carry revolvers like this? This is a Navy Colt revolver that is issued to Confederate officers, isn't it?"

"Colonel, I brought that revolver for self-defense; that is all! I am a recent graduate of the Lutheran Seminary in Gettysburg – I am traveling to my first church assignment!"

"Sergeant Major, did you find any evidence of this man's qualification as a pastor?"

"I found this here seminary diploma, a Bible, and these commentaries by somebody named Matthew Henry. These look like a preacher's books."

The colonel inspected these for himself, "Well, it looks like he was tellin us the truth! You boys can relax now. Now just to show you we hold no malice for you, Simon, let me offer you a commission in the Union Army. We need well-educated and physically fit men like you to lead our troops."

"Now you, young man, Josiah, was it? What are you about 18 years of age? Well, we can't offer you a commission but...."

"Just a minute, Colonel, I think this young fellow might have some colored blood and he won't be eligible for service in the Union Army."

The colonel was surprised, "Say, boy, take off that hat because I want to see your hair. By gum, you are right, Sergeant Major. Hair this curly would be unusual for a white man, but it's something I'd expect to see on a person with some Negro blood in his ancestry. So, what is it, son? Your mama was half white – a mulatto, and your daddy was white?"

"Yes, that is right. But you know what, Colonel? I wish we lived in a country where a person was not valued based on his race, but instead on his character!"

Hearing this, the colonel was quiet for some seconds, staring at Josiah, and then glancing at Simon, he said.

"Son, you are absolutely right. Sometimes, I forget why we are fighting this terrible war. I'm afraid many men will die before we can eliminate the evil of slavery."

"I suppose I should ask to see your papers, Josiah. But I am not going to. Of course, it might be a different story in Ohio when you cross over the state line." Then, after a few seconds of awkward silence, the colonel said, "Well, we'll be off now – Godspeed with your journey!"

"Thank you, Colonel," said Simon.

Josiah and Simon started putting their luggage back in order. "I think we lost at least forty-five minutes dealing with these Union Army fellows, but it sure beats being arrested as spies and then executed by firing squad after some quick trial."

CHAPTER SEVEN

Simon and Josiah crossed the state line into Ohio. They wanted to avoid crossing into Virginia again, so this meant taking a route that crossed the state line above the long vertical "finger" of Virginia between Ohio and Pennsylvania. When European American settlers first migrated to Ohio, there might have been as much as ninety-five percent forestation. By 1861, there were plenty of forests left.

Proceeding in their northwesterly direction toward Sandusky, Ohio, days passed without significant trouble. When it became time to quit for the day and set camp, they could pull their wagon into breaks in the woods lining the road, which was little more than dried mud with the ruts left by previous travelers' wagons. Simon and Josiah had decided that their money could be depleted if they relied on purchasing food from stores and farmers' markets along the way. They figured that they could provide some of their food by hunting game in the ample woods lining the road, so they bought a musket in Pennsylvania. This was an 1842 model single-shot smooth-bore musket.

When they purchased this used weapon, Simon said to Josiah, "You sure you know how to load and fire this gun? My father and I never went hunting, so I don't know anything about muskets or hunting and butchering game."

"Fortunately, Mr. Simon, I do. Until John Brown raided the armory at Harper's Ferry, I could take my musket and go huntin in the woods. That way my mama and me got plenty of meat for our table. But after that old crazy man, John Brown, tried to steal them guns and arm the Negroes for a rebellion, the master took away my musket. My mama and I ate more fish after that point. Plus, that old Powhattan chief, Black Bear, taught me how to make a bow and arrow. I got to be a pretty good shot with it. Come to think of it, maybe I'll make me one."

Around five o'clock one afternoon, Josiah suggested that they make camp, and then he would hunt for some small game. A clean stream ran close by, and the mules needed to drink. Josiah looked at the feedbags of oats and said, "We'll need to find a feedstore tomorrow."

Josiah succeeded in killing a rabbit, which would barely provide enough meat for the two of them. But at least they had meat that supper. The next morning, Josiah and Simon had a simple breakfast of bacon purchased the day before, pan bread, and coffee. They were just sitting down to have their meal when three young men emerged from the woods.

"Hello, the camp! Y'all have enough coffee for three travelers?

The men, little more than boys sixteen to eighteen years of age, were quite dirty with ragged clothes. One man had a revolver tucked into his pants.

"We can share some coffee with you, but we don't have extra food. Where are you fellows headed?"

"We're headed west, probably settling in western Missouri where we got some kinfolk."

"Are you planning to walk all that way? You didn't ride up on horses."

"We figure on acquiring a nice little wagon and a pair of mules shortly," said the man, pulling out his revolver and pointing it at Simon.

"Oh, so that is how it's going to be! Do any of you fellows speak German?"

"No, why are you talking about that?"

"Because these particular mules only respond to German. They won't understand you if you talk to them in English!"

"What kind of foolishness is that?"

"Allow me to demonstrate, 'Ruth and Naomi, please come here and kick these hoodlums into the next county.'"

Nothing happened. But then, when nothing happened, Simon appeared to translate it for them,

"Ruth und Naomi, komm her, um Äpfel und Zucker zu holen."

The two mules then ran into the camp, hee-hawing and kicking up their rear legs.

This was enough to distract the man holding the pistol at Simon, who drew his own revolver and fired it in the general direction of the would-be thief. "Drop your weapon, now!"

The armed thief hesitated, but then Josiah said, "Drop your weapon now! See where my musket is pointed?"

The man dropped his weapon, and Simon walked over and picked it up.

"Now, you boys best be leaving. You won't be stealing our wagon, and we'll just keep this revolver for ourselves."

"But that ain't fair!" whined the would-be thief. How are we supposed to defend ourselves on the road?"

"How could you be robbed? You got nothing to steal!" said Josiah.

Simon offered a suggestion, "There is a recruiting drive going on about three miles that way down the road. The Union army will feed you and give you clean clothes and provide you with Enfield rifles. Then you can have the adventure of a lifetime and not go hungry."

One of the would-be thieves said, "Hey, Zeb! That sounds better than starving – let's go join up!"

Their leader mumbled something under his breath and then pointed in the direction of the recruiters and said,

"OK, let's go."

"Josiah, let's treat the mules with the apples and sugar I promised them!"

"So that is why you were always speaking to the mules in German!"

"Well, to be honest, I never anticipated using the mules' linguistic abilities for this purpose, but this time it surely came in handy."

"I guess the lesson learned here is not to let down our guard so easily. Those hoodlums could have stolen our wagon and mules, and everything carried by the wagon and probably would have gotten away with it!"

"Those boys ain't gonna make much better soldiers than highwaymen," said Josiah.

"That's probably true. We don't know what their story is, why they don't have jobs, or what manner of schooling they've had. But one thing my father always told me was that hard work paid off, and there's no reason to starve in America."

"I'd agree with that, exceptin for black folks like me was starving sometimes because of the greed and cruelty of the master."

"Point well made, Josiah. Let's hope and pray that this war puts an end to slavery."

They continued on their journey without mishap until one of the back wheels broke. Simon came close to swearing because the repair was nothing they could do without the appropriate tools, and it looked like they were stuck in the middle of nowhere. Simon calmed down and said to Josiah, "Let's pray for help, that help will come our way." Then he opened his Bible and read from Psalm 91:

"Because he loves me," says the Lord, "I will rescue him; I will protect him, for he acknowledges my name. He will call on me, and I will answer him; I will be with him in trouble, I will deliver him and honor him.   With long life I will satisfy him and show him my salvation."

"OK, let's wait and see how the Lord answers our prayer."

Josiah secretly rolled his eyes a bit because he did not yet have the deep faith that Simon had, but then decided it would not hurt to wait on the Lord. And so, they waited. Then, perhaps after forty minutes of waiting for the Lord, they saw a wagon approaching them carrying a load of wagon wheels!

The driver was smiling as he pulled over next to their broken wagon and said, "I think that today, God has sent me to help you!" Then, looking at the broken wheel, he said, "Well, the quickest solution is to replace your broken wheel. I can do that here and now because I have the replacement parts and the tools on my wagon. But I'll fix this on only one condition: you come to my farm and stay the night. We'll provide dinner and breakfast. And you boys tell us your stories because something tells me you have lessons to share."

The friendly man's name was Elijah Clearwater, a man of about 40 years of age. As he worked, he told them something of his own story. He was a member of the Wyandotte tribe, most of whom were now living in Indian Territory. In 1842, the Wyandotte had ceded their land to the federal government and moved to Indian Territory in Kansas. It had been the only decision they could make to avoid bloodshed. Whites had stolen their horses and livestock, had encroached on their lands, and had killed their leaders in their sleep. They fought the federal government in the courts but lost. A few Wyandotte families of mixed blood (Indian with European) chose to remain in Ohio. These families had largely been assimilated and had been offered citizenship. Thus, culturally, they were not much different from the white citizens in the area. Elijah was himself a mixed blood, as was his wife, Samantha. They were the parents of four boys and one girl, who was the oldest at seventeen.

The two wagons driven by Elijah and Josiah drove the three miles off the highway to a small hamlet known as Marseilles.

"That white farmhouse ahead is where the Clearwater family lives. In addition to working as a blacksmith and wheelwright, I farm fifty acres and have some dairy cows, hogs, and chickens. We like it here in the country."

"Boys, you can clean up in the wash house over yonder. Then just come to the front door and knock, and probably my daughter, Justine, will let you in."

Washed and changed into fresh clothes, Simon and Josiah climbed the stairs to the front porch and knocked on the door. A teenaged girl showed them in. She smiled politely at Simon but positively beamed at Josiah, who was close to her age.

"Welcome to our home, Simon and Josiah. My father told me your names. My name is Justine. Where are you fellows headed?"

Josiah answered, "We are headed to Ontario, the endpoint of the Underground Railroad where Blacks live as free men and have established towns and prospered in their chosen occupations."

Looking a bit surprised, but not shocked or disappointed, Justine said, "But you boys are white, correct? Certainly, Simon is white. Oh!

But you…are you telling me that you are not all white but have some Negro blood as well?"

Josiah answered slowly, seemingly embarrassed, "My mother is half-and-half, and my father is a white planter. They were not married, obviously."

"Josiah, you have no reason to be embarrassed! I'm only one-half white myself, not that white is anything better or special. My other half is Wyandotte Indian."

"Simon, I understand why Josiah would want to escape to Canada and become a free man, but what about you?"

"To be honest, I am escaping the pressure to join the Confederate Army and fight for a cause I strongly oppose – the continuation of the slave economy in the South with all its cruelties. And anticipating your next question, I don't want to join the Union Army either because then I might find myself fighting against old friends–boys I grew up with–and neighbors."

Other family members had gathered around Justine, Josiah, and Simon to join the conversation. Justine's brothers, ages 8 to 14, listened attentively to the adults speaking. The oldest boy, Jefferson, asked, "Josiah, why don't you join the Union Army?"

Josiah answered, "Right now, the Union Army will not allow anyone with even a pinch of Negro blood serve as soldiers."

"You don't look black to me, not at all!"

"Maybe so, but Simon and I ran across some army recruiters on the road, and one of them caught on right away that I had some Negro blood. I guess race matters more for some folks than others. I hope someday we can get past all that."

"That might take generations, Josiah, and require a change in the minds and souls of men that only God can bring about," said Simon.

Elijah smiled and remarked, "It appears that you are a man of God, Simon!"

"Yes, well, I am a seminary graduate, but I haven't been called to a church yet."

"Well, keep praying and give it time, son. If it's God's will, that door will be opened to you."

During dinner, the family sat at a long picnic bench-type table, which had room for at least five guests in addition to the seven people in Elijah's family. As promised, Simon and Josiah shared their life stories, concentrating on the events of the past year.

"Justine said, "Josiah, did your father the planter ever acknowledge you as his son?"

"No, not once. Of course, my mother knew he was because he was the only man she ever had relations with." Looking quickly at the faces of Justine's parents, he asked, "If this conversation has become inappropriate for the children to hear, please stop me."

To which Elijah said, "Well, we don't need to hear any more than what has been said, OK?"

Josiah nodded and said, "My father wanted to keep his infidelity with my mother a secret, so he blamed the foreman, who was white, and he paid him to claim the baby as his own, and then he fired him."

"Did your mother marry someone so that you could have a stepfather?"

"No, none of the men among the slaves would touch her! They figured she belonged to the plantation owner."

"So, you never had an adult male who helped raise you?"

"Well, for a time, my Uncle Zechariah, my mother's brother, took me under his wing. But then the master hired him out to work in

Virginia's horse country. I was about 12 years old at the time. He helped teach me right from wrong and how to train horses."

"What about you, Simon? What was your family situation like?

"As you might imagine, it was very different from Josiah's. My parents were both descendants of Germans who settled in Virginia in the early 1700s. My father's family started out as shoemakers (Schuster in German), but by my great-grandfather's generation they had branched out to sell clothing, cloth, blankets, and other soft goods. My family lived above the store in Middleburg, Virginia."

"My parents were devout Lutherans and were not surprised or disappointed that I wanted to attend the Lutheran Seminary in Gettysburg. I graduated last year, but like I said earlier, I have not yet been called by a church. When Josiah and I reach Chatham, Ontario, I hope to make a living as a shoemaker, teacher, or preacher. Josiah and I have been talking about him becoming my apprentice as a shoemaker."

A pleased look passed between Elijah and his wife, smiling because they anticipated a secure future for Josiah. Then Samantha asked Simon, "Isn't there a young lady waiting for you back in Virginia? Why didn't she come with you on this flight from the coming war between North and South?"

Simon gave a momentary grimace and then said, "I was actually engaged to the daughter of a wealthy plantation owner until a few weeks ago, but this father forced his daughter to break off the engagement. He knew I opposed slavery and would not join the Confederate Army to defend a state's right to permit slavery. I asked my fiancé to come with me, but she could not for fear of being disinherited. And to be honest, I don't think she wanted to part with her fancy dresses, cotillions, and leisure-filled life."

Elijah said, "Simon, here in the North, President Lincoln has been careful to say that this war was necessary to preserve the Union, not to free the slaves. What do you Southerners say about the war?"

"Well, in the South, people believe that Lincoln is opposed to slavery and would impose abolition on the South even when he says he would rather preserve the Union than free a single slave. His record of speeches indicates that truth. The seceding states were afraid that Lincoln's Republican party would force abolition. They were resolved not to let that happen."

Josiah chimed in, "By the way, what Simon didn't tell you was that his fiancé was the daughter of my master, and so she is my half-sister, though she doesn't know it. My father won't acknowledge me as his son. No one is supposed to know that I am the son of Henry Lee Powell."

A sad smile came over Samantha's face, and then she said, "Josiah, your earthly father may have rejected you, but you have God as your heavenly father who will never reject you once you accept his son Jesus as your savior. Do you understand what I am talking about?"

"Yes, ma'am, sort of. Simon has been talking to me about his faith and accepting Jesus Christ for days on end now," he said with a slight rolling of his eyes. "But I'm not sure I fully understand everything yet."

"Josiah, study on these verses: '…if you confess with your mouth, 'Jesus is Lord,' and believe in your heart that God raised Him from the dead, you will be saved'. That is from Romans 10:9. And this: 'Whosoever, therefore, shall confess me (Jesus) before men, him will I confess also before my Father which is in heaven'. That is from Matthew 12:32."

"OK, ma'am – I will be thinking about what you said and I'm sure Simon will continue to share the Bible with me."

Mrs. Clearwater rose from the table and said, "Children, let's clear the table now!"

Justine led the way in picking up plates and silverware and was returning for a second trip when her mother whispered to her, "Justine, why don't you take Josiah on a tour of our little village?"

"Really? Do you think he would be interested in our village?"

"Honey, I think he is interested in you! And I saw the way you were looking at him."

"OK, Mother. But I am a little embarrassed about this!"

"I'm encouraging you to behave as a young lady. With all these brothers and so few girls in this neighborhood, you've become something of a tomboy."

Justine sighed, turned away from her mother, and left in search of Josiah. As it turns out, Josiah was a bit embarrassed by her attention. But gradually, he warmed to Justine, who seemed to want to hold his hand as they walked along, and so they did hold hands.

"Josiah, it seems that you are being a little shy with me – why is that?"

"Miss Justine, you must realize that I was raised as a Black slave in the South. Once I became a teenager, I could not be caught even looking at a white girl. If a white man caught me, I could be severely punished with a whipping."

"But Josiah, I am not a white girl! Well, OK – I am half white and half Indian. And don't you realize that you have more white blood than I have?"

Then Justine stood still and pulled Josiah closer to her. Then, she looked into his eyes and kissed him on the cheek. Feeling emboldened, he returned the gesture.

The next morning, Mrs. Clearwater and her daughters put on a big breakfast for Josiah and Simon. It was delicious and the guests' appreciation showed on their faces.

Josiah said, "Mrs. Clearwater, this is the best breakfast I've ever had, even better than the breakfast my father's servants would have put on for him! Thank you so much!"

"You are welcome, Josiah! But you should thank Justine because she was the head cook this morning, I just helped her a bit."

Josiah looked over at Justine and said, "Wow! Justine, thank you! You are already an expert cook. You will make a fine wife someday." As soon as he said this, both Justine and he turned red with embarrassment. Mrs. Clearwater and her husband just looked at each other and smiled.

Mr. Clearwater tried to reset the conversation, "Young men, do you intend to spend the rest of your lives in Canada, or would you consider returning to the United States eventually?"

"Well, sir – if the Union wins this war between the states, and slavery is totally abolished, I will want to return to the United States. My parents live in Middleburg, Virginia, and might need my help when they become elderly. But that won't be for some decades."

"What about you, Josiah?" Justine sat up in her chair but pretended not to be listening.

"I'm thinking I'll return to the U.S. if only because the winters are so severe in Canada."

"I'm sure the Ohio winters are milder!" said Justine, who blushed when she thought of what she had just intimated.

After the breakfast feast, the travelers loaded up their wagon for their journey to Sandusky, Ohio. Elijah had written a letter for them addressed to his cousin Nathan, who operated a steam-powered ferry on Lake Erie.

"Give this letter to my cousin Nathan, and he'll treat you well. Maybe even give you a discount on the fare."

Justine walked up to Josiah and timidly handed him an envelope with her return address on it. Inside was a letter. "Josiah, I want you to write me and tell me all about your experiences in Canada. I'll be praying for you."

Josiah shyly smiled and said, "I'll be sure to write to you! I just wish I had a photo of you to take with me."

"Then you will be pleased to find the photo in the envelope!"

"Thank you, I will cherish this picture."

CHAPTER EIGHT

"**M**an, Josiah – that Miss Justine surely set her cap for you! Her eyes twinkled at the first sight of you, and then I knew soon you would be a goner!"

"Excuse me, Mr. Simon. When did you become an authority on romance?"

Simon ignored Josiah's comeback and said, "Have you two set a date for the wedding?

Remember that I can perform the Christian ceremony as a Lutheran minister. Do you want to turn around and go back to her daddy's farm and confess your undying love?"

"Brother, your mind is still addled from falling in love with Miss Gabrielle. You've no room to talk!"

"Well, all I know is that it didn't take a half hour to walk around that tiny village – you must have been doing something else! But I won't pry…"

"Man, where do you get off implying such things?"

Simon just laughed. "It looks like you can dish it out, but you can't take it."

"Oh, shut up!"

"Well, that was rude!"

"OK, Master Simon, will you please be quiet?"

Simon started to laugh, and then Josiah soon joined him.

"OK, according to my calculations, we are about sixty-five to seventy miles from the Sandusky ferry landing. That means about twenty to twenty-five hours of driving or about three days."

"I hope that ferry is a lot bigger than that little team ferry we were on at the river crossing!"

"Oh, yes! This will be a big steam-powered ferry. We have about forty miles to traverse Lake Erie."

The last leg of their trek to Sandusky was uneventful. The terrain was flat prairie land divided into productive farms. With many railroad lines traversing the state to ship food items, Ohio was becoming the breadbasket of the United States and was the leading state in the production of corn, wheat, and wool.

Sandusky was a prosperous town of about 6,000 people. It was mid-morning when they rolled into town, and some people were on the streets. The travelers asked a local man where they could find a ferry service to Leamington, Ontario. The local man told them to go to the Jackson Street Pier and that if they hurried, they would catch the ferry that was scheduled to leave in 20 minutes.

Fortunately for Josiah and Simon, this was the ferry that carried wagons across the lake. They paid their fare and drove their wagon onto the ferry. Ruth and Naomi did not seem too anxious about this new situation, which was a blessing because if mules sense danger, they will stop and refuse to budge.

The voyage was uneventful. With a stop at Pele Island, which was about halfway across the lake, another wagon joined the passengers. Simon and Josiah introduced themselves to the driver, Mr. Augustus

Bede, who nodded and said, "I'm pleased to meet you, young fellows. You caught the ferry at the right time it seems. Earlier runs on this line are sometimes chockful of darkies escaping their masters. Damn, Quakers and Methodists buy them their tickets. The smell can be overwhelming!"

Josiah could not help asking, "Do you smell anything now?"

Mr. Bede answered, "No, just those mules and horses. They don't smell nearly as bad."

Simon caught Josiah's attention and mouthed the words, "Not here, not now," with a slight shake of his head.

Simon nodded at Mr. Bede, saying, "It was good to make your acquaintance, sir. Josiah and I have some business to discuss, so we'll take leave of you for now."

Simon indicated with a sideways nod that they should talk privately at the stern of the steamboat. Once there, Simon said, "Josiah, we are never going to escape the prejudice some people will have. What Mr. Bede said was hateful, no doubt about it. Some white people just don't want to be around black people, and they might not even know why."

"Well, I understand what you're saying because there are a lot of black people who can't stand to be around white people. They hate that white people have enslaved them, work them to the bone in the most arduous tasks under the worst of conditions, feed them poorly, take their women for sex, prevent them from learning to read, and split up their families without a second thought. Black people are tired of having to kowtow to white people, even when they are free persons. Black people are made to feel inferior to white people as if they are little more than animals."

"You know that I would never treat black people in this manner, right Josiah?"

"I know it, Simon. You are a good and kind man, and you are a faithful friend. You practice your faith. Seems that lots of white folks are Christian in name only."

"It pains me to agree! I had a thought about why so many white people dislike black people. The reason could be that they see their own selves in them. I don't think many whites would admit it, but secretly they know that the white race is not smarter or nobler than the black race. What really drives these people nuts are black leaders and intellectuals like Frederick Douglass. I heard that man speak in Philadelphia – he was beyond eloquent! He presented superbly reasoned arguments against slavery. I hope that you get the opportunity to hear him yourself, Josiah!"

"I've been meaning to ask, is President Lincoln an abolitionist like you?"

"Well, the President has said that he thinks slavery should be abolished and that all men have the God-given right to liberty and justice. But I'm afraid that the President does not yet have a high opinion of the abilities of the black man. He is afraid that if the black man were set free and continue to live here in the United States, we would find ourselves with a permanent underclass. Black people would always find themselves poorly educated and impoverished. He supported the idea advanced by the American Colonization Society that black families should be sent back to Africa to set up their own society!"

"Oh, hell! That would never work – I can tell you right now. Black folks here are Americans, not Africans. They would not know how to survive there, and probably get themselves killed by a lion or crocodile!"

"Well, the American Colonization Society founded the colony in West Africa and called it Liberia. Since its founding in 1816, 15,000 former slaves have settled there and have set up a society like they experienced in the American South. Get this – some of the wealthiest Americo-Liberians have made slaves out of the native blacks! In 1846, the Liberians declared their independence from the United States, wrote a constitution modeled after ours, and set up a democratic form of government. If it weren't for their emulation of the American southern white culture, I would think that they would be on the way to success. But they can't continue enslaving Africans from the bush without consequences. They are far outnumbered!"

"What kind of people are in this American Colonization Society?"

"Here is where it gets really bizarre! Some members are Quakers like the Rowntree family we stayed with in Pennsylvania. Some Quakers believe that blacks will have freedoms in Africa that they will never attain in America. Other members are slaveholders who are afraid of slave rebellions like the Nat Turner rebellion of 1830. They don't mind black people having a chance at freedom so long as they live in Africa."

Josiah just shook his head and said, "It's going to be a long road to freedom and equality for black people, maybe centuries if those Quakers in the ACS are any indication of how some of the most liberal white people think."

"Black folks need to accomplish remarkable things despite the encumbrances white people put on them. The black man must work extra hard and attain his goals so that white people cannot deny or ignore his abilities."

CHAPTER NINE

It took the better part of a day for the steamship ferry to cross the lake to the Port at Learnington, Canada West. Both Simon and Josiah were a bit green because, for the last ten miles or so, the lake had been choppy, and the ferry had been tossed up and down. The wind was picking up, and the temperature was dropping. A major storm was coming!

After asking a person on the street to point out the road to Chatham, Josiah and Simon set off driving their buckboard wagon to the town, which was still twelve hours away. Given the time, they would have to pull off the road and camp for a night. To their chagrin, the wind whipped up, and a strong thunderstorm blew in, forcing them off the road to find refuge under some tall oak trees. They thought that they would not be able to pitch their tent in the wind, so they laid the canvas out flat under the wagon and slept on top of it there. There was no dinner or coffee that night.

The next morning, when the storm had passed, they were able to build a fire to make coffee and cook some eggs they had bought from a farmer on the way. Simon and Josiah were damp and groggy from a night of uncomfortable sleep but at least had their coffee and nourishment.

Two days later, they drove into the bustling town of Chatham. Josiah was excited as he viewed the town.

"This place is amazing! Look at these businesses here! Black folks appear to own and operate all kinds of businesses such as grocery stores, boutiques and hat shops, blacksmiths shops, a lumber yard, an ice company, livery stable, pharmacies, folk remedies, and carpentry services."

"Did you happen to see a shoemaker and shoe repair shop? asked Simon.

"No, I can't say that I did. Maybe that's a sign from God about what kind of business we should start up. And look there, there is a 'For Rent' sign on that storefront next to the haberdashery."

"That could be a good location for our business. Let's stop by there and see if we can find out who the owner is and how to contact them."

After a down payment to the landlord, Simon and Josiah were given the keys to the property. The young men were delighted to learn that the property included a furnished upstairs apartment. The next day, they found a sign painter so that they could open for business. The sign read 'Josiah & Simon – Shoes repaired and custom-made." They found the lumber yard and hardware store to buy the supplies they would need to build worktables and a counter with cubby holes for shoes. Built into their counter was a locking drawer for their cash. By noon on their opening day, they already had four customers. Simon had Josiah do the repairs under his guidance because Josiah was apprenticing under Simon.

One evening, as Josiah and Simon were walking home after a meal at the local restaurant, a large, rough-looking man standing at the swinging doors of a saloon was observing them carefully. He was not happy to see the young men and stepped in front of them. "Good evenin, gentlemens. How are you enjoying your visit to this here town of black folk?"

Simon answered, "Good evening, sir. We like this town very much. In fact, we recently opened a shoe repair shop down the street. I came here to help my friend Josiah get his business established."

"Why aren't you white people doing your business in white towns and cities, like Toronto and Ottawa? This is a black town just for black folk who escaped slavery. Say, wait a minute, your accent sounds familiar. I bet you hail from Virginia – a nigger-hatin state if there ever was one!"

"You are correct in inferring that we are from Virginia. I came here to Canada to avoid being forced to fight for the Confederacy, and I didn't want to fight for the Union because that would mean fighting against friends and relatives I grew up with."

Reason didn't seem to make any difference to this large, belligerent man. "You ain't in the Union army because you is a coward! Let me tell you something – I hate white do-gooders like you two. I'll bet your daddies were among those white devils who went around killin black folks at random after the Nat Turner rebellion was put down in 1831. I was just five years old when a mob of white men dragged my daddy outa bed and strung him up like he was a murderer. I had to watch my own daddy die. He had nuthin to do with dat slave rebellion, but he lost his life anyway. Dat was in Jerusalem, Virginia."

The belligerent man started pushing Simon on the shoulders, but Simon didn't fall. Instead, he tried to put some distance between himself and his attacker. When the belligerent man lost his cool and ran at Simon, Simon was ready and hit him hard in his mouth, knocking out a tooth. Enraged even more, as a result, the attacker tried again to grab Simon, who side-stepped him again and landed another hard punch to the man's ear. Enraged beyond reason, the attacker succeeded in tackling Simon and hit him hard on the jaw and then stood up and started to kick him in the ribs. At this point, Josiah tackled the bigger man and landed multiple hard punches to his head. Simon had a chance to crawl away, hoping to regain some strength. In the meantime, the attacker shook off Josiah, then grabbed him and threw him into the street. He was preparing to kick Josiah in the ribs when an even larger man came running up and tackled him. The larger man then pulled the man up and hit him hard under the chin with an uppercut. The man who came to Josiah's assistance was none other than Samson, whom he had encountered in Pennsylvania. The man who had attacked Simon was terrified of Samson, who, as the village blacksmith, was easily the biggest and strongest man in the community. Samson dragged the man by the collar over to the closest horse trough and held him under for what seemed like three minutes. As Samson brought the man out of the water, he said, "Are you ready to apologize to these young men?" When it looked like he was hesitating, Samson dunked him again, and when he brought him up again, he said, "How about now?" The man sputtered out a yes. And Samson stood him up and pushed him over to where Simon and Josiah were sitting on the raised sidewalk. The man said, "I'm sorry I picked a fight with you," and then collapsed onto the street. Samson didn't bother to pick him up.

"Samson, thank you! This is the second time you rescued me. Do you recall the first time, back in Pennsylvania some months ago? I had been captured by the slave hunters and you knocked one of them off his horse with a well-placed rock!"

"Oh, yeah! That's why you looked so familiar. Rumor is dat dis thug who was beating on you two is a wanted criminal in the States. He's not just a runaway slave. He's wanted for arson and murder. He set his massa's home on fire while the fambly was sleepin, Killed everybody in the fambly, parents and chilluns."

Whereabouts do you two live? I'll drive you there on my buckboard. And I'll get my wife Esther to see if she can get you all on the mend. She's really good with her doctorin."

"We live above our shoe repair shop down the street, next to the haberdashery," said Simon.

Samson hurried off and returned with his buckboard wagon. Esther was sitting next to him, holding her doctor's bag. Samson lifted Simon like he was a ten-pound sack of potatoes and set him on the wagon. Josiah just needed a little boost. When they got to the shoe repair shop, Samson carried Simon up the stairs to his bedroom and put him in his bed. Josiah was able to stumble into his own.

Esther wrapped Simon's ribs and gave him folk medicine for pain. Concerned that he was spitting up blood, she asked Samson to fetch the medical doctor. Samson left at once for the doctor's office.

The doctor examined Simon and recommended applying ice to the injury. Internal bleeding could occur if a rib was actually broken and piercing an internal organ, but he didn't think that had happened with Simon because he stopped spitting up blood during the course of the physician's examination. Bruising was another matter. Simon would be quite black and blue the next day. Samson went to the icehouse to buy some buckets of ice. Esther and Samson spent much of the night nursing Simon, and then at midnight, they drove home in their buckboard.

As they were preparing to leave, Esther handed Josiah a slip of paper, "If Simon's condition worsens in the night, come get me at this address. You can read, correct?"

"Yes, I can read. This address is just one block over and one block down from here, right?"

"Yes, that is correct."

CHAPTER TEN

Simon's condition did not worsen overnight, but he wasn't feeling any better either when he attempted to get out of bed.

"Simon, the doctor prescribed bed rest for you, so don't even think of trying to work today. If there is a shoe that I don't know how to repair, I'll bring it up here, and you can tell me what to do, OK?"

"Well, neither can I lean over a workbench, nor can I work with these hands! When I boxed in college, we always had boxing gloves on – makes all the difference."

"Say, we didn't open yesterday's mail. You got a letter from Emily!"

"Good, I sent her a letter last week telling her about our adventure so far. I left out a lot of details – things she didn't need to know about."

Simon clumsily and slowly opened the letter with his sore hands. The letter was shorter than he would have expected. The letter read:

Dear Simon,

It was good to hear that you and Josiah got to Canada without mishap and have recently opened a shoe repair shop. It is good for Josiah to have a trade.

I regret to inform you that four weeks ago, I met a young captain in the Confederate Calvary at a special cotillion held in honor of the brave men who will defend Virginia in this war of Northern aggression. He is over six feet tall and is a wonderful dancer. He comes from a wealthy planter's family in southern Virginia. We had a whirlwind romance, and I accepted his proposal of marriage.

I am sorry that things could not work out for the two of us. I hope you come to understand that it is all for the best. I'm sure you realize that my father would never forgive you for what he considers disloyalty to your country. He says you can't expect to have a future in Virginia after the war.

Simon, you are a good, loyal, and intelligent man of faith, and I'm sure you will find the right girl someday, someone who loves you for these great qualities you possess and shares your values.

I will always have fond memories of you, and I wish you the best!

With Christian love,

Emily Howell

Simon read the letter silently, then folded it back up. Staring down at his bare feet, he said,

"Well, I can't say that this comes as a surprise. Emily has found herself a new beau. She didn't waste much time once I had left."

"Oh, brother – I'm sorry to hear that! But honestly, Simon, you gotta admit that a heavy burden has been lifted from your shoulders! You are a free man! And if I were you, I know what I would do."

"What is that?"

"I would return to the Rowntree farm and declare my love for that beautiful girl you met there, Gabrielle. And brother, I wouldn't delay. I'd write her a love letter today and get my ass down there as soon as I could."

"You sure about this?"

"Man, I wasn't the only one who could see that she was falling for you and you for her. Don't miss this opportunity!"

Simon still appeared to hesitate. To which Josiah said, "Look Simon, maybe you are thinking of that old saying that bad things come in threes. We've had two in the last two days. First, getting the crap beat out of us last night, and now that letter from Emily. If you want to wait for the third bad thing to come along before you set off for Pennsylvania, I wouldn't blame you."

"Oh, that is just a silly superstition with no basis in reality."

"We'll find out soon enough!"

Josiah was able to manage the workload on his own while Simon recovered, though Simon would check in with Josiah occasionally and lend a hand. They were doing a brisk business and finally reached a point where their business was clearly profitable.

Sometime past midnight, they woke up to the sound of an oil lantern crashing through their storefront window.

"What was that?!" Josiah excitedly asked.

"It sounded like someone threw a brick through our window."

"Wait a minute! Now I smell something burning!"

Their bedroom door was closed, so Simon warned, "If the doorknob is hot, don't open the door!"

So far, the fire had not spread up the wooden stairs, so after grabbing some change of clothing and throwing it out the window, they ran down the stairs, Simon wincing in pain all the way. Fortunately, the fire had not reached the store entrance, and they were able to escape.

Their next-door neighbor appeared carrying two three-gallon fire extinguishers. "I heard the crash and then smelled the smoke. Here, I have two fire extinguishers. We don't want this fire to spread to neighboring buildings." While the neighbor and Simon were using the fire extinguishers, Josiah ran out to yell, "Fire." But neighbors were already running to the scene with their buckets to form a bucket brigade. With the help of all these community members, the fire was put out.

The damage to their shop was significant. In addition to the wooden items that were charred, there was smoke that ruined some clothes, and there was water damage as well.

"Josiah, we can't stay in our apartment tonight. Let's take these clothes we salvaged and get a room at the hotel. Oh, but we will need some cash! I hope our cash box was truly fireproof as advertised."

"I'll go check now. I have the key in my pocket. A few minutes later, Josiah called over Simon, we were lucky – our cash was not destroyed in the fire."

"Well, I would say that God was protecting us. But look – here we are, standing on the sidewalk in our nightclothes! Let's go behind the building and change into these clothes we saved. We can't walk the two blocks to the hotel like this!"

CHAPTER ELEVEN

Faith Rowntree practically danced into the bedroom she shared with Gabrielle, then said, "Dear sister, guess who got a letter from Canada today! It is addressed to Miss Gabrielle Rowntree. Do we know anyone by that name?"

Gabrielle blushed and said, "Dear sister, will you please hand that letter to me?"

Faith said, "Oh, it is written by a Mr. Simon Albrecht. That name sounds familiar, doesn't it? Should I open it for you and read it aloud?"

"Don't you dare!" said Gabrielle who practically grabbed the letter from Faith.

"Oh, Gabrielle, please forgive me for teasing you so!"

"You are forgiven. Now, please allow me to read this letter in peace."

Once Faith left the bedroom, Gabrielle closed the door and opened the letter. She was surprised by her trembling hands and the butterflies in her stomach.

The letter read as follows:

Dear Gabrielle,

Josiah and I are well and now have a successful shoe repair shop in Chatham on Main Street. Recently, we had a couple of misfortunate events, including a fire in our shop that was quickly extinguished thanks to our neighbors. We will be back in business within a week.

Josiah has quickly become skillful in shoe repair, making it possible for me to travel and visit you and your family. It should come as no surprise to you, my dear Gabrielle, but I fell in love with you during my stay on your family's farm. You are a constant presence in my mind, and scarcely a moment goes by without me wishing we could be together. I pray earnestly that you can accept these admissions of love and longing and, in some measure, feel the same way.

Thus, when I return to the Rowntree family farm, I will ask your father for your hand and, when you are ready, propose marriage.

I am still recovering from an injury but hopefully will be able to travel in two weeks' time.

Of course, if you would prefer I not visit you, please write back and let me know.

With all my love,

Simon

Faith and her sisters then knocked on the closed door, "May we come in?"

"Yes, and I'll tell you what Simon said in his letter, which I know you are all dying to hear!"

Faith said, "Well, what did your beau have to say, if you don't mind us asking?"

"He said he loves me and wants to return here to ask for my hand in marriage!"

"He wants to marry you?"

"Yes!"

"So, what are you going to do?"

"I don't know yet!"

CHAPTER TWELVE

Simon and Josiah had spent the night in the Freeman's Hotel in Chatham after their store and apartment were set afire by an arsonist. They had just seated themselves in the hotel restaurant for breakfast when a distinguished older gentleman walked up to their table. Simon immediately recognized the man as Frederick Douglass and stood up to greet him.

"Mr. Douglass, sir, what a pleasant surprise! I heard that you were visiting our town. We would be honored to have you join us for breakfast! I am Simon Albrecht, and my friend is Josiah DeMornay."

Josiah added, "Mr. Douglass, Simon has told me about you and your important work. We indeed would be honored to have you join us."

"Young men, I was hoping to run into you this morning because last night I heard about your misfortune, and truth be told, I had been hoping to interview you even before I heard of how you were attacked by a misguided thug and then had your place of business and home set on fire by an arsonist. You see, I am touring the towns here in Canada West that were founded by escaped slaves and plan to report in the newspapers of the United States that these towns are phenomenally successful model cities. This, of course, should help dispel any misconception the white majority might have about the abilities of black people. Your story captured my attention when I heard that you (pointing to Simon) had helped a young black man to escape and establish a business. What you two are doing should serve as an example of white and black men working and living together in harmony. Forgive me, Josiah, but I probably will not mention that you apparently have more white blood than black. That might detract from my story."

"As a person with one-quarter black blood, I was black enough to be kept as a slave. But I'm not black enough to serve as your example of a successful black tradesman. I guess race will always be an issue in American society."

Mr. Douglass winced at these words, "Son, it is widely known that my father was white, and my mother was black. There are white people out there who are quick to attribute my success to my white ancestry. I meant no disrespect to your black ancestry."

"Oh, Mr. Douglass, I should not have made any fuss about it. You know best what needs to be done."

Changing the subject, Mr. Douglass asked, "What about this man who attacked you? Do you know his name? What motivated his attack?"

"We don't know his name, but the man who broke up the fight is the town blacksmith who is called Samson. He claims that the attacker had killed his master, along with his wife and children, by setting fire to their home."

"So, this man, if indeed it is the same man, has a history of violence against white people."

"He is holding onto a terrible grudge because, as a child, he saw a mob of white men lynch his father after the Ned Turner rebellion."

"But you had nothing to do with that lynching – you were not even born yet!"

"But my accent reminded him of Virginia, where he hails from, and that was enough to set him off."

"Simon, I see that you are moving slowly and stiffly, which suggests that you are still in quite a bit of pain. Let me hire a buggy and drive with you young men to your place of business and home and see what needs to be done to reopen your shop and make your apartment livable."

As they proceeded toward the shoe repair shop, Mr. Douglass made a point of saying hello to everyone he met on the street and even stopped by the lumber yard and hardware store and gently persuaded the lumberman to follow them to the shop to help them determine what was needed to repair their business. The stature of Mr. Douglass in the black community was enough to get the community's support in repairing the shop and the apartment above it. In a matter of a week, the shop was reopened for business. The cooperative can-do spirit of the community became part of Frederick Douglass's testimony about the virtuous qualities of the freed black men and women who had escaped to Canada.

CHAPTER THIRTEEN

Simon Begins the Journey to the Rowntree Farm

Two weeks had elapsed since Simon took the terrible beating on Main Street, and he was still not fully recovered. He wrote to Gabrielle to tell her that he expected he would need another two weeks, a total of four before he could travel. He made certain to tell her that this was the only reason for his delay – he didn't want her to think that he was having second thoughts. Gabrielle wrote back to assure him that she was eager to see him again but that he needed to first recover from his bruised ribs. She would wait and pray for his recovery.

Heartened by Gabrielle's reply, Simon made a special effort to make sure Josiah completed his training. There were no rules about when a person could provide services as a shoe repairman and shoemaker, but Simon had been thoroughly trained by his grandfather and had brought with him his copy of a textbook on the subject. Its contents included: Fundamental Shoe Terms, Hides and Their Treatment, Processes of Tanning, The Anatomy of the Foot, How Shoe Styles Are Made, Shoemaking and Repairing, Leather and Shoemaking Terms, and Leather Products Manufacture. Josiah had been practicing his reading and could now learn independently from the textbook.

"Josiah, you are ready now to run this shop on your own – you have mastered the fundamental skills and are on your way to becoming a journeyman. In two weeks, I will feel confident about returning to Pennsylvania. But there is some unfinished business."

"Unfinished business? We are all caught up with our repairs."

"No, I mean the unfinished business of your faith. I promised your mother I would disciple you. Has there been any change in your relationship with Jesus in these past few months? We've been attending the Campbell African Methodist Episcopal church every Sunday, and the preacher there is excellent."

Josiah sighed, then said, "To be honest, I still have my doubts. I mean, I believe in Jesus, that He was the Son of God, and died on the cross for our sins, then was resurrected on the third day. I know all that, but I just don't understand this concept of grace. I don't deserve his love and forgiveness – how can the Son of God care about what happens to me? And it seems that I should be doing something more to get into heaven."

"Well, remember – there is nothing you can do to earn your way into heaven. Only Jesus's sacrifice will cover your sins – anyone's sins – and make you righteous before God. 'All have sinned and fallen short of the glory of God.' 'But God demonstrates his own love for us in this: While we were still sinners, Christ died for us.'"

"I am sorry, but this is still all mind-boggling for me."

"Well, keep in mind that in James's epistle, we are told, 'If any of you lacks wisdom, you should ask God, who gives generously to all without finding fault, and it will be given to you.' I don't think anyone completely understands what Jesus has done for us, but I don't think Jesus requires understanding, he simply requires faith, which is '... confidence in what we hope for and assurance about what we do not see.'"

"OK, Simon. I appreciate what you have done for me and what you are trying to do now."

"And I appreciate your openness and honesty, Josiah!"

Simon had his trip all planned. He would ride with Josiah in the buckboard wagon to Learnington and take the ferry across Lake Erie to Sandusky, Ohio. From there, he would take a train south to Pittsburgh. For the last leg of his journey in western Pennsylvania, he thought he would rent a horse but changed his mind and decided to buy a horse and a saddle with saddle bags. Because he did not know how long he would stay with the Rowntree family, he thought he would buy a well-used horse; hopefully one that would not die on the way.

Gabrielle had sent Simon a road map with landmarks for Simon to follow from Pittsburgh to the Rowntree farm. Mr. Rowntree was well acquainted with the route and drew the map for him. Simon took that as a good sign because it seemed that the Rowntrees wanted to make sure he got safely to their farm.

The first three legs of his journey, i.e., Chatham to Learnington, Learnington to Sandusky, and Sandusky to Pittsburgh, proceeded without mishap, but progress seemed tortuously slow to Simon, who by this time could hardly wait to see Gabrielle again. Simon found that the last leg of his journey, from Pittsburgh to the Rowntree farm, on horseback presented the most challenges. First of all, Simon had to find an inexpensive horse and a used saddle with a blanket. Having never been to Pittsburgh before, Simon did not know where to get a good deal on a reliable horse. He walked over to a saloon and asked a few of the patrons there and got a recommendation for a stable and livery service. He also went to the largest church in downtown Pittsburgh and met briefly with the pastor of the church to see if he could recommend anyone, thinking that a church member might deal in horses. The name the pastor provided was the same as he heard with the patrons at the saloon – Donald Dunleavy – who operated a stable and livery service downtown. The Dunleavy stable was located next to the recently established (1857) Pittsburgh Police Bureau, which used the stable to house their horses for the mounted police. Simon felt this fact vouched for the proprietor's honesty.

Simon walked into the stable and addressed Dunleavy, "Good afternoon, sir. I need to buy a horse and saddle with a blanket. I don't need a fancy or fast horse, just one healthy enough to deliver me to southwestern Pennsylvania. And I must admit that I don't have the funds to pay for a horse in its prime."

"A well-used horse, you say? Well, let's see. There's Molly, who has just retired from the police force. She has new shoes and good teeth. Then there is Matilda, her sister, who is two years younger and also a police force retiree. Both are gentle mares. I can let you have Molly for $10 and Matilda for $11. A saddle with saddlebags will cost you $25, and a horse blanket $2. Altogether, your total will be thirty-seven or thirty-eight dollars, depending on which of these sisters you buy. I'll let you think about that for a bit while I visit the outhouse."

When Dunleavy left to take care of his other business, the twelve-year-old stableboy approached Simon. "Mister, I'd spend the extra dollar for Matilda. I ride these horses to exercise them a few times a week, and I know that old Molly cannot be urged into a gallop. I think she has arthritis in her knees. Matilda is in better shape and can gallop if you need her to."

"That is good advice! I just might need to gallop to get out of a storm."

"Or escape some highwaymen. Do you have a gun?"

"Well, yes. I have an 1851 Colt."

"Just so you know, my father was held up by some bad men just a few weeks ago. He was returning home after a trip to York on business. He wasn't seriously hurt but got a tooth knocked out when he got into a fight with the bad guys. He didn't have much money on him, so they stole his horse. He had to walk nineteen miles home!"

"How far do you think I could ride Matilda in a day?"

The boy looked away in thought for a few seconds and then said, "Well, that all depends on how fast you go and what the terrain is like. But I know this, as a police horse, she was used to a ten-hour shift, with breaks, of course, and most of the day, she would lope along at about four or five miles an hour."

Dunleavy returned and asked, "Well, son, which fine Equus caballus will you purchase?"

"Latine loqueris. Admiror linguam Latinam extra seminarium audire! Oh, you speak Latin. I am surprised to hear Latin outside of the seminary. Well, I think Matilda will be just fine. I'd like to pick her up first thing tomorrow to begin my trip."

"Why yes, I do speak Latin. There's a long story behind that! In the meantime, we'll have your new friend ready with a fresh blanket and a well-broken-in saddle with saddle bags. And tell you what, I'll toss in two bags of oats and a brush. She's used to being brushed down every night."

"Where do you plan to spend the night, young man?"

"I thought I would find an inexpensive hotel."

"No need for that, son. Come stay with me and the missus. We have a guest bedroom, and we will provide dinner and breakfast."

"That would be greatly appreciated, sir!"

Simon experienced his first good meal and comfortable bed in many days, or so it seemed. The Dunleavys had lost their only child, Patrick, to a cholera epidemic some years earlier. Since then, they opened their home to numerous young people in transition. Simon noted that if their son Patrick had lived, he would be the same age as he was today.

At the dinner table, Mrs. Dunleavy asked Simon about his destination and the reason for his journey. Simon told the Dunleavys much of his story, of how he had escaped Virginia with Josiah with hopes of starting a new life in Canada where there was no slavery. He related the story of the slave hunters and how he had been taken to a Quaker family farm to recover from a beating he had suffered at the hands of the slavers.

"This Quaker farmer had six lovely daughters, and I fell in love with one of them. Her name is Gabrielle – and I really hope that she feels the same about me. I am going back there now to see if she will allow me to court her."

Mrs. Dunleavy (Kaitlyn) smiled broadly and said, "This story sounds familiar, doesn't it, Donald? Do you want to tell it or should I?"

"You consistently complain that I embellish the story, so perhaps you should tell it this time."

"Very well, I will!"

"I was the second oldest of six sisters, all beautiful blondes except me, a redhead. In Ireland, as in many parts of the world, the oldest daughter should be married off first. But in the case of the Muldoon sisters, there was little hope of that. Connie Muldoon had a fiery temper and a quick tongue. She was quite particular about whom she would marry, as I suppose a girl should be. But it was carried to the extreme with Connie. And here she was at twenty-five and not married."

In the meantime, I had all sorts of suitors. There was a pharmacist, a train engineer (a new occupation back then), and an officer in the

King's army. But none of them could hold a candle to my favorite, a young seminarian."

"I was that seminarian, a candidate for the Catholic priesthood. And I didn't even know this young lady was interested in me. But it might not have made any difference because I was about to commit myself to a life of celibacy. Of course, once I met these six sisters, I immediately had second thoughts about that decision. One, in particular, caught my fancy, the redhead!"

"There was still the obstacle of my older sister, Connie, who turned away most suitors. That is why Donald had his cousin, Sr. Anna Marie, talk with Connie. She put it into Connie's mind the possibility of the sisterhood. Was she not satisfied with any man because they fell short of our good Lord, Jesus? To make a long story short, Connie decided to enter the convent."

"And that meant that I, as the second oldest, could accept an offer of marriage! But there was a problem – my father's uncle, who was childless, had died and left the entire estate to my father. Well, the uncle's farm was a world away, in America. Seeing an opportunity to improve our standard of living, my father sold his own little farm and planned to move us that great distance."

"In the meantime, I had just quit the seminary with the hopes of formally courting Kaitlyn. With her moving to America, and me not having two nickels to rub together, I was afraid the love of my life was slipping away."

"But I was determined to follow her! Her ship had already sailed, leaving Ulster in the summer of 1830. I could not afford passage, but I heard that I could sign on as a crewman on a ship bound for America. Fortunately for me, the first mate, who did all the hiring, was a good Catholic. He hired me as a cook's helper. And for this, I was relieved because I didn't think I could climb the tall rigging of a sailing ship. I am deathly afraid of heights!"

"My family left for America about two weeks ahead of Donald. In New York, we bought a covered wagon and a team of mules to transport the family and our household goods to Lancaster, Pennsylvania. The only address I could leave for Donald was the Muldoon Farm, two miles due north of Lancaster."

"I still didn't have much money, so I had to find a means of transport that didn't require a ticket. I found a small wagon train leaving New York City where the people were especially kind to me and invited me to travel with them. They didn't speak much English, just some form of German. I think they called it Plautdietsch. Fortunately for me, their destination was Lancaster, Pennsylvania! It was practically a straight shot west from Philadelphia."

"When we arrived in Lancaster, my new friends, who called themselves Mennonites, wanted to help me find the Muldoon farm. They were impressed to see that I carried a Bible among my few possessions. They knew I was Catholic – and you know the Catholic Church had persecuted them in Europe – yet brought me to another farm on a Sunday where they were going to hold a worship service. This service was quite unlike anything I had experienced before, and it was all in High German. I didn't understand a word of it, but I could see that they were genuinely worshipping God. After the service, they had a potluck type of dinner and spread the word about me, wanting to find the Muldoon farm. One fellow happened to know where the farm was and offered to take me there in his family buggy!

"I was sitting on our front porch steps when that little black buggy pulled up, and Donald stepped out! I had been praying that he would find me, and I was overjoyed to see him!"

"Son, we told you this story because there is a lesson in it for all believers. When you commit your quest to the Lord, he will guide your path. He will overcome great distances, poverty, and differences in religion when you are faithful."

"Amen to that!" replied Simon.

CHAPTER FOURTEEN

Simon Begins the Final Leg of his Trek

Simon mounted his steed and began the slow journey to southwestern Pennsylvania. He was relieved to find that Matilda was a smooth-riding horse, not too bumpy. But his ribs started to hurt him anyway as the day progressed. By evening, when he stopped to set up camp, he cringed with pain as he dismounted. A soft bed would have helped him to rest and recover, but of course, he did not have one. He rolled out his bedroll and used Matilda's saddle as a headrest of sorts. Simon made a fire for his coffee and then dined on a sandwich Mrs. Dunleavy had packed for him. In his mind, he thanked both God and Mrs. Dunleavy for her thoughtfulness.

The remainder of Simon's journey was a lesson in perseverance. To minimize the stress on his body, he kept Matilda's pace at a walk of about four miles an hour. Sometimes, he would have Matilda break into a lope of about eight miles per hour, but not for long distances because the pain to his ribs became too much to bear.

Simon found an inn in a small city called Waynesburg where he could sleep one night and get dinner and breakfast. Sleeping in a real bed had been a rare luxury on this journey, and Simon did not jump out of bed at dawn as he had planned, but he did find his way to the breakfast table on time. The food was delicious, and Simon lingered a little longer at the table than he planned, having a second cup of coffee and a second muffin. The proprietors of the inn turned out to be a Christian couple who took an interest in the young man reading his Bible and sat down with him.

"Hello, young man! We are Hans and Gertrude Stuerm, the owners of this inn. We noticed you reading your Bible, and we were wondering if, by chance, you were a minister of the Word."

"Well, I am a recent graduate of the Lutheran Seminary in Gettysburg and have a Master of Divinity degree, but I have not yet been called to a church."

"The reason we mention this is that our pastor over at Saint John's Lutheran Church is going to retire soon."

"Gertrude, I think he actually retired some months ago."

"That's not nice, Hans! He has just slowed down some, as anyone his age is likely to do!" "Well, anyway, as Pastor Schmidt's retirement approaches, we hope to call a new pastor. "Perhaps you would like to serve as a guest preacher – we can make that happen if you so desire. Will you be staying in this area?"

"I would be interested in preaching some Sundays. I will be staying at Mr. Rowntree's farm."

Hans replied in a whisper, "The Rowntrees? I know them through the underground railroad."

"Yes, that is the family. They are a pious Quaker family."

"And how do you know them?"

Simon then related a short version of his story, including the part about Gabrielle.

"Son, we will be praying that this works out for you!"

Simon arrived at the Rowntree farm just before the dinner hour. The youngest of the Rowntree sisters had been watching for him, and when she realized it was Simon, she shrieked and ran inside the house, shouting,

"He is here, he is here! Professor Simon has returned!"

Joseph and Elizabeth Rowntree walked out of their home to greet Simon. Joseph noticed Simon wincing as he began to dismount and hurried over to help him.

"What happened to you, Simon? Were you mugged by some highwaymen?"

"No, I had a safe and uneventful journey. I am still recovering from the beating Josiah and I had at the hands of a man who didn't like my Virginia accent."

Elizabeth said, "Why would he be upset with your accent?"

"He said his father was murdered by a white mob in Jerusalem, Virginia, in the aftermath of the Nat Turner Rebellion in 1831, even though he had not participated in the violence. My attacker was just a small boy when he watched his father being dragged out of their home and murdered."

"Oh, this world is such a violent and sinful place!"

"When did this beating occur?"

"About five weeks ago now."

"Well, we won't ask you to do any physical labor on the farm."

"But if it is agreeable to you, I could resume lessons for the girls."

Joseph and Elizabeth exchanged nods, and then Elizabeth said, "That would be greatly appreciated, and we are sure the girls would enjoy having their 'professor' back!"

"We were just setting the table for dinner when you arrived. So please join us now after you wash up a bit from your journey."

After dinner, Simon and Gabrielle had some private time together, walking along the perimeter of the farm. Simon nervously took Gabrielle's hand and, with some trepidation, asked Gabrielle, "Have you given any thought to my offer of marriage."

Gabrielle was choosing her words carefully, "Oh, I have been praying about this since before you left. It's just that I am so confused about what I am feeling. This is all so new to me. Simon, for the first time in my life, I have a family with a Godly mother and father, and sisters! Honestly, I just want to stay here and enjoy this experience for a time."

"I thought that you were one of six sisters! So, you are saying you are unrelated?"

"Right, we are not related by blood. Instead, I was adopted." Gabrielle realized that her words would lead Simon to the mistaken inference that she was adopted as a small child.

"Well, God certainly placed you with the best family he could find."

"Well, no, it was not like that exactly. You see, I came here just a few days before you and Josiah showed up. I was part of a group of runaway slaves that stopped at this farm because it is a station on the underground railroad. The conductor for the group asked Mother and Father if I could stay here with them because my sprained ankle was slowing down the group and putting them at risk of being caught. The Rowntrees immediately agreed to take me in. They told me that I could stay with them as long as I wanted to."

"How could you have been a slave? It is obvious that you are not Black."

"This might surprise you, but one-eighth of my ancestry is Black – my maternal great-grandmother was Black. My other ancestors were English, Scottish, and French in origin. But by Louisiana law, any person with just one drop of Negro blood is a Negro, and if they are born to a slave, they themselves are slaves."

Simon did not know what to say, but he felt that he should say something. What came out was rather lame,

"You must have been a domestic servant in one of those giant plantation mansions."

"If I had been holding that job, I might have never escaped. No, the job imposed on me will no doubt shock you. I was a 'Fancy Girl.' I lived in bordellos, first in New Orleans and then in Lexington, Kentucky. I was one of several quadroon and octoroon girls whose job was to provide sexual favors to wealthy plantation owners and other self-proclaimed gentlemen. My very own father sold me into this life when I was just sixteen! I never saw any money – it all went to my father and the bordello operator. Now, does this truth affect the way you think about me?"

Simon had stopped and just stood there stunned, looking down at his feet. In those moments, Gabrielle thought, He is just like all the other men I have met. He is standing here thinking I am not good enough for him.

Then he said, "Before you told me your story, I had decided that you were the most beautiful, intelligent, and kind woman I had ever met! And now I add to that the strong impression that you are an overcomer! With God's help, you can overcome any adversity that comes your way. Oh, Gabrielle, now I love you even more strongly!"

Now, it was Gabrielle's turn to be stunned. "You really love me? We knew each other only a matter of days before you left! How do you know what you are feeling is love?" She felt even a bit annoyed and angry that he would talk this way. She was unprepared to fall in love after all she had suffered from men in the bordello.

"Simon, I think you are still pining away for that Southern girl who had been your fiancée. You are probably still hoping that after this war, she will take you back."

"No, that will never happen – in a letter, she told me that she is now engaged to a Confederate officer from a wealthy plantation family. To be honest, all I know is that I enjoy every moment with you. And now that I have experienced this feeling, I don't want to leave without you."

Gabrielle took Simon's hand and was silent for perhaps ten seconds, then she said, "My feelings are complicated and confused. I might be falling in love with you, but I just don't know, Simon! This feeling is all so new to me, and I am confused by it. Perhaps if I experience the love and care of a normal but pious family for a time, which I've never had before, I'll understand what I am feeling. Of course, this means I can't go with you at this time. Perhaps in some months or even years, I'll be ready."

Simon said, "I think I understand, and I want you to experience the love of a family – everyone deserves this, and I certainly would not want to take it from you. If it is all right with your parents and with you, of course, I would like to continue my visit here until I wear out my welcome. If I must move on without you, I will return to Canada. But I will write you letters every day if that is all right with you. And then someday, I hope to return here and, well…we will figure out what we should do."

Then, the two would-be lovers leaned toward each other to kiss. As they ended the kiss, Gabrielle said, "I will be praying for wisdom for both of us!"

Their stroll had taken them back to the farmhouse, and Elizabeth Rowntree then appeared on the porch and said, "Your sisters could use your help in the kitchen with the dishes, Gabrielle."

Gabrielle smiled politely and then said, "I will go there now, Mother."

As she left, Elizabeth's eyes followed her until she was out of earshot, and then, turning to Simon she said, "So, Simon – now that you know Gabrielle's background, do you still love her?"

Simon blushed some and said, "I didn't know anyone knew of the degree of my affection for her! Was it that obvious?"

Elizabeth smiled and rolled her eyes, and said, "Simon, when you are near Gabrielle, it seems as if there is nothing else or no one else in your universe! Yes, a blind man could see you were in love!"

"But can she love me in the same way?"

"Simon, right now, she is just confused. I think she has romantic love for you, but she needs time to recover from her ordeal as a 'fancy girl' so that she can completely trust you and her own feelings. Besides, the Rowntree family needs her for a time – we feel that God has given her to us to love and to heal! Does that make sense to you, Simon?"

Simon gave a thoughtful nod and said, "Yes, that makes perfect sense, and thank you for inviting Gabrielle into your family!"

CHAPTER FIFTEEN

Simon was enjoying his time living with the Rowntrees and courting Gabrielle. He wrote to Josiah in Chatham, Canada West, telling him that he planned to stay with the Rowntrees through the Christmas season. Josiah wrote back, saying that he had their business well under control and there was no compelling reason for Simon to return at this point. In the meantime, the church council offered Simon the opportunity to be a guest preacher at the Lutheran Church in Waynesburg, and after preaching there twice, the church council offered him an associate pastorship under Pastor Schmidt. This was a part-time position, making it possible for Simon to continue the role of 'professor' for the Rowntree girls.

Back in Chatham, Josiah continued with his shoe repair business and was doing well financially but feeling restless. He felt frustrated with not being part of the war to win his own people's freedom. Then, after the first of the year in 1863, Josiah ran into his acquaintance, Frederick Douglass. As it turns out, Mr. Douglass was in Chatham recruiting for the new Massachusetts 54th regiment, which was entirely composed of black soldiers commanded by white officers. He had intentionally sought out Josiah at the shoe repair shop, having been impressed with his character.

Josiah looked up from his work as the bell rang when a customer entered the store. To his surprise, he saw that it was Frederick Douglass walking up to the counter.

"Mr. Douglass! I wasn't expecting you back here – what brings you to Chatham?"

Douglass, smiling, said, "Greetings, Josiah. A couple of things. One is to see how you and Simon were getting along in your business, and from the look of things, I can tell it is thriving! The second is recruitment of black ex-patriates for the Massachusetts 54th regiment of infantry soldiers, which is going to be an all-black unit commanded by white officers."

"All black soldiers? Will they be a true fighting regiment or a support regiment behind the lines?"

"The 54th will be a true combat regiment! My own two sons are enlisting. Josiah, I can't emphasize strongly enough that this regiment must exceed the white man's expectations. The prevailing attitude in the North has been that black troops would not be smart enough to learn the skills they needed, that they would be lazy, and would be cowards running away in the face of battle. You young men must prove them wrong!"

"I want to enlist in the Army, Mr. Douglass, but I need to know what Simon would want to do with this shoe repair shop. It was all his money that got us set up in business."

"Oh, Simon is no longer here?"

"No, he is living in Pennsylvania. He is courting a Quaker girl we met on our way north."

"So, you need a person to take care of the business for you while you are off soldiering."

"Yes, we would either sell the business or pay an employee's wages."

"Well, then we should begin looking for a suitable partner for you. You can train the person and then hire him as your replacement while you serve in the Army. I will help you find a suitable man for the job.

I recommend against trying to sell your business because I don't think many people in these parts have that amount of cash on hand. Besides, you might want to return to your business when the war ends."

Josiah sent a letter to Simon describing his plan to enlist in the 54th Massachusetts all-black regiment and hire a man to run the shoe repair business while he was away at war. Simon wrote back, saying that he thought Josiah should proceed with his plans.

In a second letter, Josiah wrote Justine. He told her that after the first of the year (1863), he would be enlisting and that he would like to visit her before leaving for Boston. As soon as she received his letter, Justine sent a telegram to him inviting him to her parents' farm for Christmas. Josiah felt relieved to find a man qualified as a cobbler and he hired him right away. He was confident in hiring this man who was thirty years old, married, with two small children. His skills, along with his steady commitment to family, told Josiah that he would work out just fine.

Josiah decided to reverse the route Simon and he had taken from Marseilles, Ohio, to Chatham, Canada West, with their mule team pulling the buckboard wagon. This meant taking the ferry across Lake Erie. Taking the ferry resulted in a 150-mile trip, which Josiah figured would mean almost four days traveling at five miles per hour. Given that it would soon be winter, snow might mean a slower trip requiring more than four days.

Josiah packed some changes of clothes, some canned foods, and his single-shot musket. He didn't have reason to expect trouble on the trip, but he was going to be prepared. On the coldest of nights, he would try to find lodging at an inn, which meant he would have to pass as white. Even in the north, there were restrictions on where a colored person could stay the night and even buy a meal.

The trip proceeded without mishap until one evening outside of a saloon/eatery in Sycamore. Josiah had finished his meal and was walking to his wagon and mules when a black man called out to him from the shadows, "Excuse me, suh – could you do a brother a favor and see if you can buy some food for mah fambly? I have the money to pay for it, but these white folks won't sell us any food! I have a wife and two small chillun, and we ain't eaten nuthin all day."

Josiah could see the family standing mostly in the dark by their covered wagon. The father told Josiah that they were headed west where they hoped there was greater opportunities for a man with his blacksmithing skills.

"Well, what can I get for you?" Josiah asked.

"Dey has some whole roasted chickens in there dat would be enough for us. We has water to drink. You can take dis here bag and put the chicken in it."

"OK, wait here and I'll go get you a chicken."

The cook had some chickens roasting and Josiah bought two. The cook gave him a curious look, and asked,

Didn't you just eat here?"

"Yes, I did, and it was really good. I'm buying these for a friend and his family."

Josiah paid for the chickens and left the eatery. As he left, two rough-looking characters got up from their table and followed him outside. They were staggering drunk.

Josiah walked over to the father and handed him the bag with the chickens. The man wanted to hand him some money in payment, but Josiah waved him off, "I am a business owner – I have plenty of money. Please just accept this as a gift."

As Josiah turned to go back to his wagon, one of the ruffians grabbed his arm. "Say boy – did you buy those chickens for that colored family we seen lurking around here?"

"I bought these for a friend – why does that matter to you?"

"We want to keep this town white. We don't want shiftless colored people coming around here. Wait a minute, you yourself are kind of colored, ain't you?"

Josiah hesitated for a moment, but then said, "You insult me! I am Egyptian, and if you know what's good for you, you'll apologize and be on your way!"

Not entirely convinced of their error the two ruffians mumbled something and started to return to the saloon. But Josiah felt guilty about denying his black ancestry, and he turned back to the thugs and said, "Well, truth be told, I am not Egyptian. I am one-fourth black and three-fourths white. But don't worry, I'm not planning to stay in this town if you two are the kind of the people who live here."

The thugs looked at each other, and one said, "Did he just insult us?"

Josiah just shook his head and drove off with his wagon in search of the inn the proprietor of the eatery had told him about.

The entire Clearwater family poured out of the house when Josiah's wagon pulled onto their lot. Elijah and his wife Samantha were the first to the wagon to greet Josiah. "Welcome home, son!" said Elijah, smiling broadly. "Yes, welcome home dear son," said Samantha.

Josiah was touched by the warm reception, but at the same time, he was confused. What did I do to merit this treatment? Justine walked up to Josiah and hugged him. She smells good, no --actually wonderful, thought Josiah. The hug was longer than he expected, and he could feel himself stirring. Oh, dear Lord, I hope this isn't showing!

Samantha was smiling, "Josiah, you don't have to sleep in the barn anymore. Justine, please take Josiah around back and show him where he can stay."

Justine, smiling, took hold of Josiah's hand and said, "OK, come with me!" They left by the back door and to Josiah's surprise found a spanking new cabin. "This is our guest house! It has two rooms and a kitchen. The bed is all made up – I did it myself this morning – and there is firewood for the stove and fireplace that my brothers provided."

Then without another word, Justine wrapped her arms around Josiah and kissed him on his mouth. Josiah, initially taken aback, thought, Hmm, this is nice! And then he enthusiastically responded to the kiss.

Justine pulled back and said, "I should get back to my mother. She might be wondering what is going on back here!"

"OK, I'll put my clothes away and go get washed up for dinner."

"The boys have already taken care of your mules. So come in when you're ready."

At this point Josiah wondered what kind of situation he had walked into. He shook off the thought, and when he was ready, he returned to the farmhouse.

Justine was coming out as he approached the back door. "There you are -- we are ready to have dinner."

At the dinner table, once everyone was seated, Elijah said, "Josiah, would you please offer our thanks to God in prayer?"

His stomach started to do somersaults – Are they trying to check on my credentials as a Christian? Josiah snapped out of it and said, "Yes, sir. Let us bow our heads in prayer." Josiah thought, I can do this – I just need to imitate what Simon has said in offering the grace. "Lord Father in Heaven, we come before you in thanks for this good food, our good health, and the prosperity of this farm. We pray for the needy and hungry in our nation today, Lord and ask you, dear Father, to show us how we might respond to their needs. In Jesus's precious name, we pray, Amen."

"Josiah, that was a wonderful prayer! Thank you!"

The dinner was the best Josiah had had since he had left his mother's cabin where they ate the leftovers of the Howells' meal. The discussion at the table was mostly about his experiences with Simon in Chatham and the visit by Frederick Douglass. The boys wanted to hear more about the fight with the brute, and the rescue by Samson, and then about the attempt to burn down their business and home by probably the same man. Samantha and Elijah wanted to hear more about Frederick Douglass, whom they admired as a crusader for justice. Having been oppressed as Wyandotte Indians in their youth, they admired men who fought for the natural rights of all people.

Samantha had the children clear the table after dinner while Elijah smoked a pipe with Josiah on the porch. It was chilly but not as cold as it usually was for Christmas Eve in Ohio.

"So, young man, you will become a soldier and fight for our republic and for the rights of all men. Certainly, for the black people who are now enslaved, but really all men, for if one race or one people can be enslaved, then any group can be enslaved."

"Yes, sir! That is what Mr. Douglass talked to me about."

"Then, son, assuming you are not killed in this war, what are your plans?

"Well, sir, I am not sure what my plans are at this point. But I think I should visit my mother in Loudon County, Virginia. I'm assuming she is still the housekeeper for the Howell mansion on the plantation. And after that, I could return to Chatham, Canada, and resume my shoe repair business. Or I could stay in Virginia and help my former master rebuild his plantation. Of course, only for fair wages, this time!"

"Josiah, I honestly doubt that the white Southerners will ever treat black people as anything but second-class citizens. Resentments will run deep among the white people who saw their beloved menfolk killed and their farms and plantations ruined by Yankee soldiers. No, it's not going to be pleasant for black folks for a long, long time."

Josiah was silent for a while as he considered what Elijah was saying. "I suppose I could ask my mother to come stay with me in Canada. Oh, but she would not like the cold winters at all."

"May I offer a suggestion? You could settle here in Ohio on this farm. It's not much colder here than Virginia, and if your mother wanted to live with you, we could add a room or two onto the cabin."

At that moment, Samantha walked onto the porch and said, "And of course, if you and Justine are truly in love, then the two of you could marry and live in the cabin."

The pipe dropped out of Josiah's mouth at that thought, and Elijah and Samantha just smiled and chuckled.

"Oh, come now, Josiah – I've seen how the two of you look at each other! Your mutual attraction is no secret," said Samantha.

"But if I lived here, how would I make a living?"

"Well, you could continue your trade as a cobbler and shoemaker, but then expand into other leather goods such as saddle bags, saddles, leather aprons, holsters and other things."

Josiah was getting nervous about these ideas he was hearing from Elijah and Samantha. Does Justine love me? How can that be? I haven't spent more than a few hours with her.

The Clearwater family turned in early, and parents and children were in bed by nine o'clock. Josiah was grateful for that because it had been a long and exhausting day. He got into bed and blew out the oil lamp on his nightstand. It was chilly now, just above freezing, and he was grateful that the Clearwaters had found two blankets for this bed.

Several hours passed, and he was sound asleep when an uninvited visitor slipped into his bed.

Very cold feet touched his legs, and Josiah woke with a start and stupidly said, "Who's there?"

"It's me, Justine, nothing to be frightened of. Please roll over and hold me, it's cold tonight."

As if in a dream, Josiah did just that and then thought, hey, what is going on here?

As if Justine could sense his confusion, she said, "OK, I just thought we could have a private moment together cuddling, nothing more. Just remember my father's brother will be at our house for Christmas dinner, and he is an ordained minister. If we were to get married, we could fall asleep cuddling every night – wouldn't that be nice?" Then she kissed him on the cheek, slid out of the bed, and walked out the door.

Oh, good Lord – what have I gotten myself into?

Simon continued as a teacher to the Rowntree sisters and as an associate pastor, not giving much thought of doing anything else until June 29, 1863, when news came of General Lee's invasion of Pennsylvania. No one knew this yet, but Gettysburg would become perhaps the most important battlefield between the Union and Confederate armies in this development of the war. Simon and Joseph Rowntree were in Waynesburg picking up supplies at the general store when they first heard the news. The Army of Northern Virginia was moving northward toward Harrisburg, and the usual cast of farmers was standing around the store entrance speculating on Lee's objective.

"Oh, Lee won't stop at Harrisburg. His ultimate objective must be Washington City!" said one old farmer, his hands high on his suspenders.

"Then, it is unlikely that he will turn west towards Pittsburgh, and Waynesburg is not in any danger."

"Naw, Lee will try to penetrate deep into Pennsylvania and draw the Union forces out of Virginia, which has suffered greatly in this war. But mark my word, General Hooker and his army will get between Lee and the Capital, and he won't get further than Gettysburg."

"Mr. Brown, you speak with remarkable confidence about military matters for a farmer!" said one of the farmers, smirking.

"I'll have you know that I have been a student of war since I was a young pup! At the tender age of fifteen, I ran away from home to fight the British in the War of 1812!"

"Well, then. I suppose that qualifies you to be an armchair general!" mocked another farmer in his fifties.

Joseph touched Simon's shoulder. "Come now, young man, let us return to the farm with our supplies."

With their buckboard wagon loaded, they began their ten-mile journey home. Joseph noticed that Simon was quiet for most of the trip and said, "Simon, has all this talk of the invasion of Pennsylvania made you reconsider your decision to stay out of the war? I would understand if you felt you should defend Gettysburg after spending several years there in college. It's bad enough that your home state has been so brutally torn up by the war. Now it seems that your adopted home could suffer the same if Lee isn't turned back."

"Well, Mr. Rowntree – I doubt that I'll ever become a Quaker, but your Christian pacifism has rubbed off on me. I will never be a soldier. But I can't help but think I could do something to help the people in the war zone, both civilian and soldier, as a minister of the Word."

"You know, of course, that soldiers need the Lord as much as any civilian, perhaps even more so. Could it be that the Lord is calling you to serve as a chaplain? I think especially the wounded and dying men in the hospitals need to be encouraged and comforted by the word of God."

Simon's eyes met with Joseph Rowntree's eyes but neither man spoke further of this matter. Simon spent the remainder of the trip back to the farm in silence. He pondered the matter in his mind, what does the Lord want me to do? Is it right for me to sit out this war entirely, or does He want me to minister to the wounded and dying soldiers caught up in this terrible war?

The next day was Sunday, and Simon was due to preach the sermon at St. John's Lutheran Church in Waynesburg. The text that day was Matthew 25: 34-40:

"Then the King will say to those on his right, 'Come, you who are blessed by my Father; take your inheritance, the kingdom prepared for you since the creation of the world. For I was hungry, and you gave me something to eat; I was thirsty, and you gave me something to drink; I was a stranger, and you invited me in; I needed clothes and you clothed me, I was sick, and you looked after me, I was in prison and you came to visit me.'

"Then the righteous will answer him, 'Lord, when did we see you hungry and feed you, or thirsty and give you something to drink? When did we see you a stranger and invite you in, or needing clothes and clothe you? When did we see you sick or in prison and go to visit you?'

"The King will reply, 'Truly I tell you, whatever you did for one of the least of these brothers and sisters of mine, you did for me.'"

Simon hesitated for a few moments after he read this passage to the congregation. Is this God telling me to be charitable to the needy and even to my enemies? Then he snapped out of it and began his sermon.

"In this passage, Jesus is calling us to be charitable to needy persons we encounter in our daily lives, because this is what Jesus Himself would do. And Jesus so identifies with the needy, that we are in effect ministering to Jesus."

"So, just how far does this command extend? How should we behave towards our enemies? Right now, at this point in history, our enemies are our own countrymen in the rebelling states of the Confederacy. Should we be charitable toward them? I believe that the Union will eventually put down the rebellion; then what? We will be one reunited country. Oh, I know it's hard to imagine this right now, but someday, commerce will reopen between the north and the south, and the south will have to reconstruct itself. Then our southern states, our former enemies, will be our neighbors again. Now, please turn to Matthew 5: 43-48, which says:

"You have heard that it was said, 'Love your neighbor and hate your enemy.' But I tell you, love your enemies and pray for those who persecute you, that you may be children of your Father in heaven. He causes his sun to rise on the evil and the good and sends rain on the righteous and the unrighteous. If you love those who love you, what reward will you get? Are not even the tax collectors doing that? And if you greet only your own people, what are you doing more than others? Do not even pagans do that? Be perfect, therefore, as your heavenly Father is perfect."

"I believe that Jesus is calling us to love our Confederate enemies right now before the war ends. This might seem like an impossible thing to ask of us, but if we pray about what to do in earnest, Jesus will show us the way. And the occasion to show love toward our enemies might happen sooner than you think! It looks like soon a great battle will be fought in our state some miles to the east."

Perhaps it was no coincidence that a colonel in the Union Army was visiting the church that Sunday morning. He was dressed as a civilian, so no one knew that he was a soldier. As he filed out of the sanctuary with the other congregants, he shook hands briefly with Simon and said,

"Pastor Albrecht, might I have a brief word with you?"

"Yes, I would be pleased to talk with you. Allow me to finish here, then we can talk. Please wait for me in the sanctuary."

The colonel was very direct in his conversation with Simon. "Pastor Albrecht, I am Colonel Wilson of the Pennsylvania militia. I believe that we met a couple of years ago on the highway. After an unfortunate moment of suspecting you to be a Confederate spy, I apologized and offered you a commission in the Pennsylvania regiment I was raising. I came here to present a new offer to you, not realizing that the young man I was seeking was the same man I had met two years ago on the highway!"

"Let me understand you, Colonel – did someone recommend me for this commission?"

"Yes, indeed! One of your professors at the Seminary, Dr. Fromm, strongly recommended you for the position of chaplain. He knew that you had taken this associate pastorship because you had written to him. He related to me that you might be feeling that you should do more in the war effort."

"Well, yes – there are moments that I feel some guilt for not doing my part, which would really be God's work."

"Son, I can empathize with you. A bullet at Antietam rendered my left arm paralyzed, and I was left-handed. Since then, I have served in a non-combatant role. I don't feel I am as useful as I was with two arms."

"But back to my proposition – you would be directly commissioned as a 2nd Lieutenant in the Chaplain Corp. Your appointment would be for ninety days, after which you may sign up for another ninety days if both you and your commanding officer agree this would be good for the Army and yourself."

"But where would I serve? I don't want to be some great distance from my adopted family – I know this is selfish of me, but…"

"There's no need to be overly concerned with that issue, son. You will stay in this theater of the war, not moving far from Pennsylvania. Your first assignment will be at the military hospital in Gettysburg, which is where I expect our next great battle to occur, where wounded soldiers, both Union and Confederate, will be treated. If the Union soldiers survive but still need more hospital care, they will be moved to a more permanent military hospital. If they are Confederates and can be moved, they will be transferred to Fort McHenry in Baltimore."

"Colonel Wilson, I will need a day to discuss this offer with my Quaker family. Will you be staying in Waynesburg?"

"Yes, until Tuesday, I will have a room at the inn run by the Stuerms."

"Then I will see you by Monday evening."

"I hope your answer will be yes. If so, we will leave together on Tuesday morning. We will be driving a buckboard wagon the one hundred and eighty miles to Gettysburg."

Simon spoke with Joseph Rowntree first. Mr. Rowntree responded in a nuanced Quaker manner: "Simon, this could be God calling you for a special purpose. You would not be fighting, and your ministry would be to wounded soldiers on both sides of this terrible war. You should pray on this then decide."

Simon's next conversation was with Gabriella. Tears welled in her eyes as she listened to Simon. With her emotions overwhelming her,

Gabrielle said, "If you think this is God's will for you, then who am I to protest?" Then, she initiated a kiss with Simon, and it quickly became passionate. "Simon, I'm sorry that I have kept you waiting while I sorted out my feelings. I am ready to say now that I love you with all my heart, and I want to marry you!"

Simon was surprised by Gabrielle's admission. His heart pounded fiercely for joy, and then he said, "Oh, how I love you, Gabrielle! My love for you knows no bounds, and I want you to be my wife more than anything else. I can't imagine loving another woman more than I love you. But let's do this right." And with that, Simon went down on one knee and took Gabrielle's hand, "Gabrielle, will you make me the happiest man in the world and be my wife?"

"Yes, of course! I want you to be my husband more than anything else!"

"I'm sorry that I don't have a ring for you at this time," Simon said with some embarrassment.

"Not to worry, Simon – Quaker girls do not wear wedding rings. It is one way to give a testimony of simplicity."

"I see. A simple life is a Godly life."

"Simon, we can get married when you return from your ninety-day enlistment as a chaplain. I want to have a traditional Society of Friends (Quaker) wedding. The wedding would be conducted as part of a regular worship meeting of the Quakers without a lot of fanfare. I don't know all the details – we should talk to my mother and father, who will know what we need to do."

"So, you think of the Rowntrees as your parents now? And this traditional Quaker wedding will honor them?"

"Yes, it is a way to give back to them some of the love they have shown me."

"The Rowntrees are certainly worthy of your love…and mine because they demonstrated God's love for you, and that has helped you immensely!

"Back to the present – I must depart for Gettysburg early Tuesday morning. I already told Pastor Schmidt of my plan to serve as a chaplain, and he gave me his blessing and wished me well. Now I must ask for your blessing, dear Gabrielle."

"You have my blessing, Simon! And I will pray for you every day, for your success in ministry, and for your safe return to me. We are promised to each other now, and I intend to hold you to your promise!"

That evening at the dinner table, Gabrielle made an announcement, "Mother, Father, and all my wonderful sisters, I am happy to announce that Simon and I are to be married!"

Joseph and his wife were smiling and mouthed their congratulations. Their words would not have been heard because of the joyous outburst from the sisters rushing over to hug Gabrielle. The youngest sister, Joy, who was just thirteen, put her arms around Simon and kissed him on the cheek, saying, "You don't have any younger brothers, do you?" Simon laughed and said, "No, but in a few years, I will be sure to send you a young man who merits your attention, that is, if I ever find one!"

Joseph said to Simon, "Gabrielle just told me that she wants a traditional Quaker wedding, and her mother and I are delighted. But you must be mindful of the approval process that the Society of Friends requires for engaged couples."

"First of all, the couple choosing to have a traditional Quaker wedding must send a letter of intent to marry to the clerk of their meeting. The clerk will read this letter at the next monthly meeting for business, and the Friends attending this meeting will appoint a two- or three-member clearness committee to discuss marriage with the couple. The committee will pose questions addressing potential issues couples can encounter in marriage and discuss the spiritual nature of marriage. If the clearness committee approves of the proposed marriage, the couple may marry in the manner of Friends."

"This is a more thorough process than the Lutheran Church has!"

Joseph went on, "In the society of Friends, there are no ministers and thus no officiants at weddings. Instead, Friends believe that they are married by God, and the couple declares their intentions before God and those gathered. The marriage is merely "witnessed" by those attending the meeting. Back in 1669, the founder of the Society of Friends, George Fox, said, 'For the right joining in marriage is the work of the Lord only, and not the priests' or the magistrates'; for it is God's ordinance and not man's; and therefore, Friends cannot consent that they should join them together: for we marry none; it is the Lord's work, and we are but witnesses.'"

Simon announced his decision to enlist as a chaplain at the noon meal on Monday. The girls were surprised and upset at the thought of losing their beloved professor. Then, when they heard that Simon would need to leave the next day for Gettysburg, they flew into a fury of preparing food baskets he could share with the colonel on their journey.

Early the following morning, Colonel Wilson arrived at the Rowntree farm. The family was just finishing their breakfast when they heard the buckboard wagon pull up. There were some tearful goodbyes, and Mr. Rowntree offered a prayer for Simon's safe travel and success as a chaplain. Then, as the family retreated into their home Gabriella came forward to embrace Simon and give him a long-lingering kiss. The colonel looked away, but when it looked like the kiss was not going to end any time soon or might even develop into something more serious, he cleared his throat and said, "Lt. Albrecht, it is time for us to depart. We have one-hundred and eighty miles to travel."

After some minutes on the road, the colonel looked at Simon and said, "I can see why it was so hard for you to say your farewells – your girl is surely a beauty. And I would wager that she is quite a prize for her intellect, faith, and hard-working attitude as well. Well, I think we have reached a turning point in this war, and your ninety-day appointment will fly by, and the war might even end before you have completed your ninety days. I predict Gettysburg will be a decisive win for the Union, and down south, under General Grant, we will score another decisive victory in Mississippi. Yes, sir! The Union army will win this war by next year at this time at the latest!"

Simon didn't give much credence to the colonel's predictions, but he didn't try to make a counterargument. Instead, he turned the conversation to what his duties would be in Gettysburg.

"Well, first, you will be partnered with a man with considerable experience as a chaplain. You might have to attend a lecture or two about the traditions in the Army, ranks, and positions in the Army, and the officer's code of conduct. But given the number of wounded soldiers in this great battle from both sides, there will be separate facilities for the Union heroes and the Confederate rebels. Your training and orientation period will be short, and you must get up to speed quickly."

"So, I will be ministering to both Union and Confederate soldiers in the hospital – which group will I serve first?

"To the best of my knowledge, you will be ministering first to the Union soldiers and then the Confederate soldiers. But be flexible – the head chaplain will have orders that you should follow."

CHAPTER SIXTEEN

Simon completed his orientation and training in his first week at Gettysburg. His alma mater was not accessible because the battle was still raging there, so he stayed behind the battle lines near the large tents serving as military hospitals. Armed guards patrolled the hospital tent holding the wounded Confederates just in case some brave rebel soldier felt he could escape.

Simon's tent was set up near the area designated for officers, but it was close enough to the hospitals that he could hear the moaning and groaning of the wounded soldiers throughout the night. The pitiful sounds were so terrible that he could not sleep. Instead, he rested on his cot praying for the injured, pleading with God for relief, comfort, and healing, if possible, for these poor men. Giving up on sleep, Simon got dressed, grabbed a lantern, and walked to the hospital tent where Union soldiers were hoping for recovery or, sometimes, in the most desperate of cases, death.

The first soldier he ministered to had to have an arm amputated. He was awake, moving his head from side to side and softly moaning. He didn't immediately notice Simon's presence, but when he did, he asked,

Lieutenant, are you a chaplain?"

Simon responded, "Yes, I am. I'm here to pray with you and offer whatever comfort I can."

"Father, I'm sorry to carry on so with my moaning. I should be thanking God for sparing my life, but now I am worried that without my right arm, I won't be able to provide for my wife and child. When I left home to join the regiment, we had just found out that Elfriede was pregnant with our first child." The young man looked up at Simon with tears welling up in his eyes. He didn't look to be more than eighteen or nineteen years of age.

Simon didn't bother correcting the young soldier telling him that he wasn't a Catholic priest. His purpose with this young man was to comfort him and encourage him for the road ahead.

"First, please tell me your name. I am Lt. Simon Albrecht."

"Father, my name is Private Friedrich Klausmeier of Prairie du Chein, Wisconsin.

"What kind of work did you do in Wisconsin?"

"My family runs a dairy farm. The farm was my grandfather's, and now it is my father's."

"So, you work with your father on his farm. He can't be much more than forty years old – if so, he has a lot of years that he can still work. Are you his only son?"

"My father is forty-two, and he is healthy and strong. And I am his only son. I have four younger sisters."

"Well, Friedrich, it seems to me that your father would be capable of taking on some extra work while you recover and regain your strength. But I have a feeling that there is something else that worries you?"

"My wife – how can she love a cripple like me?" Tears were streaming down his anguished face.

"Young man, Elfriede will be so relieved just to have you back. She will welcome you home and love you just as you are. God will help both of you through this trial. But you must pray. Jesus said that he will be with us to the very end. Here are some Bible verses to meditate on: Joshua 1:9 says, 'Have I not commanded you? Be strong and courageous. Do not be afraid; do not be discouraged, for the LORD your God will be with you wherever you go.' And Isaiah 40:31 says, 'but those who hope in the LORD will renew their strength. They will soar on wings like eagles; they will run and not grow weary; they will walk and not be faint.'"

"I don't know, Father, I've never been a man of faith…"

"Well, it is time that you consider putting your faith in Jesus! Jesus is calling you. He's given you a second chance to live your life in faith. The minie ball that pierced your arm, could have pierced your skull, and we would not be having this conversation."

"Friedrich, Jesus said in Revelation, 'Behold, I stand at the door and knock. If anyone hears My voice and opens the door, I will come into him and dine with him, and he with Me.'"

"Well, Father, if that is true, I hope we might serve him something better than this Army food!"

Simon had to chuckle at Friedrich's quip, "I hear that the grub is even worse in the field – but Jesus was just talking about sharing your thoughts, hopes, fears, etc. He loves you and wants you to realize that fact."

"Father, I know there are other soldiers you will want to visit tonight, but can you come back tomorrow and help me write a letter to my wife?"

"I surely can! I'll stop by in the morning."

Simon ministered to six other wounded Union soldiers that night, then returned to his tent. He ended up getting about three hours of sleep that night but was grateful nonetheless for the opportunity to serve.

On July 3rd, the ill-fated Picket's Charge resulted in about 7,000 casualties for the Confederate Army. Robert E. Lee had believed that after Confederate attacks on both the left and right flanks of the Union lines on July 2, Union General Meade would reinforce his defense lines there and neglect the center. But Meade anticipated Lee's intended plan and the Union Army council of war decided to reinforce the center with additional soldiers and cannons.

On the morning of July 3, the Confederate Army launched a heavy artillery bombardment to soften the Union forces and take out its artillery. But it was ineffective. The Confederate infantry assault involving 12,500 men in nine infantry brigades had to advance three-fourths of a mile across open fields under heavy Union artillery and rifle fire. Some Rebel soldiers were able to breach the low stone wall protecting the Union defenders, but most did not. The Confederate army suffered more than fifty percent casualties. This was a catastrophic defeat for Lee's army, and they had to retreat to Virginia. The invasion of the North came to a halt.

Simon was among several chaplains ordered to minister to the wounded Confederate soldiers who had been captured. He ministered to several wounded rebel soldiers before he came to the cot of Captain Beauregard Hammer of Virginia, who had a leg amputated above the knee.

"Say, Lieutenant, you don't sound like you are from the North. Do I detect a Virginia accent?"

"Yes, Captain. I am from northern Virginia. And you?"

"My family owns a plantation in Southern Virginia. So how did a Virginian find himself in a Yankee uniform?"

"That is a long story, but the short version is that I could not bring myself to defend the practice of slavery, nor could I take up arms against friends and relatives in the Confederate army."

"I have to admit that it was for simple conformity that I joined this fight. I don't have any hard opinion about slavery – it is just a matter of time before it will be outlawed in the U.S. anyway. Like most civilized nations. But another reason for joining the Confederate cause was the splendid officer's uniform! The ladies just swooned over a gentleman in this fine gray dress uniform!"

The captain's smile suddenly turned into a grimace of pain followed by a loud groan. Then, through gritted teeth, "Oh, pardon my outburst, Lieutenant. I just had a terrible shooting pain in my leg that is no longer there!"

"Oh, I've heard of that phenomenon – it's called phantom limb pain. Most amputees suffer some degree of phantom limb pain."

The wounded officer was panting hard at first, and then gradually, the panting lessened in intensity. "OK, the pain is subsiding now. My God, what am I going to do? My fiancée once told me I was the best dancer in Loudon County – what is she going to think when I return home with a pair of crutches and an empty trouser leg? Will she still want me as her husband?"

"I think that she is going to be relieved just to have you home. If she is the right woman for you, she will stay by your side. Tell me what you would do if your fiancée had a carriage accident and lost a leg? Would you love her any less?"

Captain Hammer looked up at Simon, eyes moistening, "OK, I get your point!"

"Where is your fiancée staying? Is she at your parents' plantation?"

"No, she has been staying on her parents' plantation near Middleburg. Her father won't be returning home – his head was blown off by a cannonball on July 3rd! The colonel and I had grown close over the months. He was like a father to me because my own father died when I was just a lad of five years. So, you see, I am mourning both the loss of my leg and a dear friend."

"Good Lord, I am so sorry for your loss! Were you nearby and see this happen?"

"Yes, I ran over to where his body was lying just to confirm it was him and pray over him. But seconds after reaching him, another cannonball came and struck my leg, shattering it. There was no hope of saving it, so the surgeons told me."

"Did you see his face to confirm it was your colonel?"

"Lieutenant, no one even tried to collect the pieces of his head! So, I identified him, not by facial features, but by his billfold."

"Good grief, then death was instantaneous! Listen, before I move on to another soldier, I want to leave you with something you should start thinking about. It is found in the gospel of John: 'But to all who did receive him (accept Jesus as their savior) who believed in his name, he gave the right to become children of God, who were born, not of blood nor of the will of the flesh nor of the will of man, but of God.' And then this from Jeremiah: Despite your terrible injury and loss God has plans for you, 'Plans to prosper you, not harm you. Plans to give you hope and a future. And when you seek me, you will find me, when you seek me with all your heart. I will let myself be found by you.'"

"Thank you, Lieutenant. I will reflect on these words. Say, could you do me a favor and mail this letter?"

"Yes, I can do that."

And then he saw the address on the envelope: Emily Howell, Howell Plantation, Middleburg, Virginia. Unknowingly, Simon had been ministering to Emily's new fiancée! With this discovery, Simon did not say anything to Captain Hammer about his past with Emily. There didn't seem to be any point in revealing this fact. He simply resolved to pray for the best for the engaged couple.

CHAPTER SEVENTEEN

After several weeks of ministering to wounded Union and Confederate soldiers alike, the recovering Confederate soldiers were transferred to Fort McHenry in Baltimore, which had become a prison and commonly referred to as the Baltimore Bastille. Simon was redeployed as well to serve both the Union garrison and the so-called hospital for Confederate prisoners.

The commanding officer gave the officers an occasional day off, and during his first free day, Simon decided to visit his relatives' home, where he had spent some weeks during the summer as a boy and teen.

Finding the home, Simon climbed the stairs to the front porch and used the door knocker. The woman answering the door was the maid, Esmerelda, a free black woman about fifty years of age.

"Yes, suh – what can I do for you?" Then, more excitedly, "Is that you, Master Simon? Oh, I was afraid I would never see you again!"

"It is good to see you too, Miss Esmerelda!"

"What's dis, are you telling me you is a soldier now?"

"Well, not exactly. I'm wearing the uniform of a U.S. Army chaplain."

As he said this, his aunt Sarah and, to his surprise, his mother, Ingrid, rushed into the room. Ingrid screamed for joy and ran up to

Simon to hug him. "Oh, Simon – I have been so worried about you! Why didn't you write?"

"But mother, I did write – I sent you a letter every two weeks or so!"

"I suspect that our postmaster decided to discard those letters rather than permit any comfort to the family of a traitor – I'm sure that is how he thinks of you. The postmaster is known as a Yankee hater," said Simon's father as he walked into the room.

Simon's mother was crying now, "Son, after we posted that statement you wrote, our business began to decline, and people started to treat us coldly."

"Things got so bad for us that I began withdrawing our savings from the bank until it was empty. We figured we would have to move away from Middleburg. One night, two weeks after the Confederates' loss in Gettysburg, a mob decided to burn down our store and home. Mother and I were able to escape unharmed, but our business was left in ruins, and nearly all of our personal belongings were destroyed. I managed to save my shoe-making and repair kit. This might come in handy if we are to start all over!"

"Pop, I am so sorry for putting you and Mom through all this trouble!"

"Simon, it isn't your fault that these people destroyed our home. You did the right thing and followed your conscience. Only they are to blame for what they did!"

"Your father is right! We don't blame you for the evil these people did. I'm speaking of people we thought of as friends, customers of our store, maybe even members of our church. Knowing what kind of people live in Middleburg makes us want to move and find a new place to live and work," said his mother.

"Mom, you will find people who will do evil things anywhere you go."

"Yes, but these particular people did evil things because you did the right thing as a Christian," replied his mother.

"Simon, didn't Jesus say, 'Blessed are those who are persecuted because of righteousness, for theirs is the kingdom of heaven. Blessed are you when people insult you, persecute you, and falsely say all kinds of evil against you because of me?'"

"Yes, that is recorded in the gospel according to Matthew! We can expect persecution as Christians when we do what Jesus would command us to do. So where do think you will settle? Here in Baltimore? Or further north or out west? Or maybe Pennsylvania? By the way, my really big news is that I am engaged to be married to a Quaker girl I met in Pennsylvania. She might want to stay close to her parents and sisters, so I might be moving to the Keystone State."

Simon's mother almost shouted, "Oh, that is wonderful news! Is she a farm girl who has some home-making skills? Oh, I really hope so – that last girl would never be able to take care of a family."

"Yes, she lives on her parents' farm in southwest Pennsylvania and shares the household chores with her five sisters. When my tour of duty ends in three weeks, I'm returning to Pennsylvania, and we will get married. I was going to tell you about her and invite you to the wedding in a letter home. Now, it looks like the letter would have been undeliverable. At this point, we haven't set a date."

"We will look forward to that wonderful day!" said Ingrid.

CHAPTER EIGHTEEN

An ominous appearing letter was delivered to the Howell mansion addressed to Mrs. Martha Howell. It had been sent from the desk of General Robert E. Lee, commander of the Army of Northern Virginia. Martha Howell carried the letter over to her writing desk and opened the letter with shaking hands. The letter confirmed her worst fears:

Dear Mrs. Henry Lee Howell,

It is with the deepest regret that I must inform you of the death of your husband, Colonel Henry Lee Howell, this past July 4 near Gettysburg, Pennsylvania.

Henry Lee fought valiantly during this great battle, and throughout his service, he was an inspiration to every soldier he commanded. He was well-loved and respected by his men and by his fellow officers as well.

Your husband was buried at a military cemetery in Gettysburg along with several thousand other brave soldiers of the Confederacy.

I will be praying for your peace and comfort in this period of grief and mourning.

Your Faithful Servant,

Robert E. Lee, Lieutenant General,

Commander, Army of Northern Virginia

Some minutes later, Nancy De Mornay, housekeeper and mother of Josiah, found Martha Howell lying on the floor next to her writing desk. She had fainted at the news about her husband, and now, as Nancy tried to revive her, she was not responding.

Nancy ran to the front porch to shout for help, and just as she stepped onto the porch, Emily pulled up in front of the house in the family carriage driven by an ancient slave, Tiberius.

"Oh, Miss Emily – your mother has fallen to the floor and is not responding to my attempts to revive her! It could be a stroke or heart attack!"

Emily turned to Tiberius and said, "Hurry now back to Middleburg and fetch old Dr. Johnston. Tell him it is an emergency and that he needs to come with you to tend to my mother, who has had a stroke or heart attack! Do you have all that, Tiberius?"

"Yes'm, Ah'll go fetch the doctor right now without delay!"

In the meantime, Emily ran to her mother's side, still on the floor. Nancy had placed a small pillow under her head and was gently wiping her face with a wet washcloth. Emily knelt beside her mother and spoke to her,

"Mother, the doctor is on his way. Oh, please wake up, Mother!"

Turning to Nancy, Emily asked, "What was she doing when she fainted?"

"I'm not certain, but I think she had just read this here letter," holding out the letter informing the family of Colonel Henry Lee Howell's death. Emily took the letter from Nancy and quickly read it. Then, setting it down, Emily began sobbing. "My daddy is dead. Killed by the Yankees!"

An hour later Dr. Johnston was dropped off at the entrance to the mansion and climbed the stairs to the second-floor bedroom of Martha Howell as fast as his wobbly 79-year-old legs would go.

Martha was now in her bed, placed there by a male slave named Archie. Dr. Johnston examined his patient carefully and queried his patient, "Martha, can you lift your right arm? Yes, good. Now, can you lift your left arm? Not working?"

Dr. Johnston stood up slowly from his bedside chair and gently led Emily away from the bed. "Your mother has had a heart attack and a stroke. No doubt the shocking news of your father's death is responsible. I'm afraid there is no medicine for this – the best we can do is to keep her comfortable the best you can. Recovery will be slow. I will stop by tomorrow to check on her and provide more instructions on how to care for her and aid in her recovery. She is not in any danger of dying, but would you like me to ask Pastor Jennings to pay a visit?"

"Yes, Doctor, thank you," Emily said in almost a whisper. Then tears started anew as she thought of her mother's long road to recovery, widowed and partially paralyzed at just forty-five years of age. And then she thought of how she would ever manage the plantation without her father now dead and the overseer away at war. Surely, my fiancée will return soon and assume these duties.

More bad news came the next day, though Emily thought at first it was just another love letter from her fiancée, Captain Beauregard Hammer, but it was postmarked from Gettysburg, Pennsylvania. Her hands trembled, knowing that her fiancée had been with her father at Gettysburg. She unfolded the letter and read it with tears welling in her eyes:

My Dearest Emily,

I delayed sending this letter until I was assured by the authorities here that the news of your father's passing had already reached you. I am so sorry that your father died in battle, but he died a hero's death. He was struck by a Yankee cannonball and died instantly. I was close by him on the battlefield and as I knelt beside him, another cannonball came and shattered my left leg. The doctors, who were Yankees, by the way, because I had been captured, told me they could not save my leg and amputated it. As I write this letter, I am resting on my cot in a Yankee hospital tent. The pain comes and goes and sometimes it is severe and appears to be coming from the limb that had been amputated! They call this phantom limb pain. I learned this from a young Union chaplain who was ministering to us wounded Confederate soldiers. The curious thing was this young chaplain was a lieutenant in the Union army, though he had a Virginia accent and was from Loudon County. He said he graduated from the Lutheran Seminary here in Gettysburg. I don't recall his name, but he was a good and kind man of the cloth.

Emily, I'm sorry that I won't be able to dance with you at the cotillions when I return. The Union army will likely release me when I can be safely transferred home, but I don't know when that will be. At first, I was worried that you would not want to marry a cripple, but the chaplain said that was nonsense, that you would be relieved just have me return alive. After all, he said I would not love you less if you had lost a leg in a carriage accident.

I thank God that I am alive, and I ask you to pray, as I am, for my recovery and our future together. I can't wait to see you and hold you in my arms again!

With all my love, Beauregard

Once again with tears welling in her eyes, Emily folded the letter and placed it in her Bible, at Jeremiah chapter 29. Then she noticed verses in chapter 29 where she had penciled in the date she had first read this chapter and had underlined the comforting verses with pencil.

"For I know the plans I have for you," says the Lord. "They are plans for good and not for disaster, to give you a future and a hope."

"And you will seek Me and find Me when you search for Me with all your heart. I will be found by you."

Then she remembered that she had underlined these verses in the spring of 1861, when her father had forced her to end her engagement to Simon Albrecht. The chaplain Beauregard had met must have been Simon Albrecht. She thought, we must have a small world and a big God! He knows what we need before we can articulate our fears or desires. She smiled at the thought of Simon's kindness in ministering to Beauregard. He must have known that Beau was her new fiancée. After she prayed for Beau's recovery, she prayed for Simon too. That he would find a woman who could return his love with equal intensity and depth.

CHAPTER NINETEEN

Josiah was adapting well to his new life as a soldier. He quickly learned to stand at attention and salute, to march in step, and to present arms. Then, when the new soldiers began their combat training, the sergeant marveled at Josiah's marksmanship with his Enfield rifle.

"Private De Mornay – where did you learn to shoot the rifle so well?"

"Sergeant, I am from a Virginia plantation. The owner used to let me go hunting with one of his old muskets. I guess I got pretty good at it."

"Do you have any other special talents or skills the Army should know about?"

"I know horses because I spent several years working in Virginia's horse country; and I know how to repair and make shoes – that is how I made my living in Canada these past two years."

"How about reading, writing, and arithmetic?"

"Yes, I have all those skills – I was taught by a young seminary graduate."

"Well, this company needs someone with your skills to serve as quartermaster."

"Quartermaster? But Sergeant, I signed up for combat!

"Don't worry, you can be both a quartermaster and a combat soldier! And quartermaster comes with a promotion to corporal and if you do your job well, sergeant's stripes won't be far behind."

"OK, where do I sign up?"

"Just report to me after the morning formation."

Josiah left the sergeant with a new bounce to his step, thinking, I'm on my way up, now ain't that something!

His interaction had been with Sergeant Morris of St. Louis. When he looked for this sergeant the next morning, there were two sergeants waiting there by the sergeants' table, presumably for Sergeant Morris. The two sergeants happened to be Sergeant Major Henry Lewis Douglass and Sergeant Frederick Douglass, Jr.

Sergeant Major Douglass was the first to speak. "You must be Private Josiah De Mornay. We heard a lot about you from Sergeant Morris. Before that, we heard about you from our father, Frederick Douglass. He was pleased that you took his advice and enlisted in the 54th Massachusetts Infantry Regiment."

"I might not be educated or even smart, but I know a wise man when I meet one, and your father is the wisest man I'll ever meet!"

The Douglass brothers chuckled and said, "We say amen to that, brother!"

"Say, if you don't mind me asking, Sergeant Major, but why didn't the army make you a lieutenant?"

"Josiah, you won't find a single Negro officer in the U.S. Army. The commander of this regiment is Colonel Robert Gould Shaw, a real gentleman, a soldier who was already wounded at Antietam. I'm pleased to be serving under him. My father says that Negroes must prove to the white population that we are smart enough, disciplined enough, and brave enough to serve as soldiers. What white people have conveniently forgotten is the bravery and success of the Rhode

Island regiment in battles leading up to and including the conclusive battle of Yorktown."

"Are we going to have the opportunity to prove ourselves?"

"You can count on it, Josiah! In fact, soon, we are going to load up on a transport ship and sail south. Our destination is Fort Wagner, where there is a heavy artillery battery overlooking Charleston harbor, and Fort Sumter, where this terrible war began. Our objective is to take Fort Wagner!"

On the day of their departure, the 54th Massachusetts regiment proudly marched through the streets of Boston to the harbor and loaded up on the transport ship Demolay. Cheering on the soldiers were about 20,000 people lining the narrow streets. Josiah was exhilarated by the support he felt from the Bostonians, but this feeling soon left him, and his stomach started to churn with fear and doubt. Will I be courageous under fire? Lord, please help me to be a brave soldier and do my part in this battle!

"Hey, Sergeant Major Douglass, how long will we be at sea? This is my first voyage on a sailing ship!"

"This is the first sea voyage for nearly everyone! We will be at sea for at least four or five days. It's more than a thousand miles to Charleston from here."

"When we make land, we'll form up and ready ourselves for battle. This battle will not be easy. The 54th has been given the honor of leading the charge on the fort. I have been studying the layout of the land from maps. We will have to advance on the fort through a narrow strip of land, which means we won't have the advantage of superior numbers. If Johnny Reb is smart, they will have artillery to cut us down. I don't mean to scare you, Josiah, but I want you to be mentally prepared for what we could be facing!"

"Gee, thanks, Sergeant Major. I think I will spend some time in prayer now – the good Lord knows we will need his help! Are you going to address the troops and tell them about this?"

"I will first check in with the colonel. He might want to do this himself and make an inspirational speech."

On July 18, 1863, the battle began when Union troops launched an assault on Fort Wagner, a Confederate stronghold on Morris Island, South Carolina. The 54th Massachusetts was part of a large assault force, and its soldiers were tasked with leading the charge against the heavily fortified fort. The regiment was composed mostly of free black men from Massachusetts, along with some former slaves from other states.

The attack on Fort Wagner was a brutal and bloody affair. The Union troops were met with heavy resistance from the Confederate defenders, who rained down artillery and musket fire on the advancing soldiers. Despite the overwhelming odds, the soldiers of the 54th Massachusetts pressed on, charging towards the fort with bayonets fixed.

Colonel Shaw led the charge, urging his men forward even as he himself was struck down by enemy fire. When Josiah witnessed Colonel Shaw being struck down, he was filled with a rage he had never known before. He was one of the first among the soldiers of the 54th Massachusetts who continued to fight on, scaling the walls of the fort and engaging in hand-to-hand combat with the defenders.

Josiah was bent on killing the first Confederate soldier he encountered as he cleared the wall of the fort. But then he stopped in his tracks when he recognized the Confederate soldier he was facing.

"Good Lord, Amos Clifton – is that you? Without a second thought, the Confederate soldier, Amos Clifton, turned his musket around, and instead of stabbing Josiah, he clubbed him on the forehead and knocked him out. The young Confederate soldier, it turns out, happened to be an old friend of Josiah back in Loudon County. They had gone fishing together as small boys, and he couldn't bring himself to kill him. With his eyes welling up with tears, he dragged Josiah to the rear, where orderlies dragged him to the hospital tent for captives.

The battle ended in defeat for the Union, with the soldiers of the 54th Massachusetts suffering heavy losses. Of the roughly 600 men who participated in the assault on Fort Wagner, 272 were killed, wounded, or captured. Among the dead was Colonel Shaw, who was buried in a mass grave with many of his fallen soldiers.

Despite the defeat, the bravery and sacrifice of the soldiers of the 54th Massachusetts were widely celebrated. The regiment became a symbol of the courage and determination of black soldiers during the Civil War, and its soldiers were praised for their willingness to fight and die for their country despite facing discrimination and oppression at home.

As the 54th retreated to their camp, the non-commissioned officers began a tally of the living soldiers. The rest were assumed to be either dead or captured. Sergeant Major Henry Lewis Douglass had been seriously wounded, and after the field medics did what they could for him, he was transferred in an ambulance wagon to a Union field hospital. Before he was carted off, the Sergeant Major grabbed the sleeve of his brother, "Brother, find Corporal De Mornay!"

Once the ambulance started on its way, Sergeants Frederick Douglass, Junior, and Morris walked through the camp making their tally and were becoming increasingly alarmed when they did not find their young friend, Josiah. Sergeant Douglass said to Sergeant Morris,

"Brother, we haven't seen hide nor hair of Corporal De Mornay anywhere in this camp!

"Well, Sergeant Douglass, that could mean he was killed in battle, wounded and captured, or he decided to desert the Army!"

A young soldier passing by overheard their conversation and said, "Ah can assure you that Josiah was not kilt, and he did not run away either! I saw him hesitate when he came face-to-face with a Rebel soldier who was about to kill him. Then Johnny Reb, himself, hesitated for a second or so, and he turned his weapon around, and butted Josiah's head with the rifle stock. Josiah was knocked cold."

The sergeants looked at each other and Sergeant Morris said, "Maybe they recognized each other, and had been friends as children. I've heard of this sort of thing happening!"

"Then Johnny Reb decided not to kill Josiah but to knock him out and take him captive!"

"What are the Confederates gonna do with all these black prisoners of war?"

"I think that out of vengeance, the Confederates will kill the majority of them – they will view these blacks as the cause of all the Southerners' troubles, as destroyers of their way of life. And even if they don't think along these lines, they will likely think that these former slaves have tasted freedom and can't be trusted to submit themselves to white authority again. They would be afraid of them! The few submissive prisoners they find will be auctioned off as slaves! The Confederate government needs the money raised from the sales!"

Sergeant Morris wiped his brow, and looked up to the heavens, and said, "Lord, please be with Josiah and all our comrades in arms who are now prisoners of war. Protect them and bring them back to us in one piece. Please do not let them be killed nor subjected to slavery again."

"I should write to my father tonight for tomorrow's mail call and tell him what happened to Josiah. He became quite fond of the young man, and he probably knows who to contact with the news among his friends in Canada and Ohio."

"If you know where your father is right now, a telegram with the news would be many times faster!"

"Yes, that's a great idea!"

CHAPTER TWENTY

Josiah woke up with a splitting headache and nausea. As he painfully opened his eyes, he found himself in a pen with fifty other black soldiers, now all prisoners of war. "Where the hell am I?"

A man with his arm in a makeshift sling said, "You is a prisoner of war, just like the rest of us here. We got captured during our assault on Fort Wagner. We fought bravely, all of us did, but we lost that battle. Now we stuck in this pen like animals."

"Dat's all we are to these crackers! Next thing you know dey be selling us in an auction just like livestock. You can hear dem now getting the chains ready for us," said another soldier.

Josiah was already feeling nauseous from his concussion, but this conversation made his head pound anew. *Ah can't go back to bein a slave agin. Oh, sweet Jesus -- I am already reverting to a slave's manner of speaking – Lord please help me now!* Josiah's circumstances were leading him to engage in fervent prayer, more so than he had ever before.

Frederick Douglass stared at the telegram he held in his hands. His heart was heavy because he felt responsible in a way for Josiah's predicament. Reason told him that he should not feel guilty in the matter, but his emotional response, which he usually kept at bay, was getting the better of him. The telegram from his sons in the 54th

Massachusetts had taken some days to reach him, and now he was worried for Josiah. He had heard that the Confederates were auctioning off some of their black prisoners of war as slaves, sometimes making a half-hearted attempt to return runaway slaves to their white masters, and sometimes simply executing the blacks who were proving too rebellious to serve any good purpose of the Confederacy. Mr. Douglass was well familiar with Josiah's back story that he had been a slave of Colonel Howell, Josiah's biological father, whose daughter Emily was once engaged to Simon Albrecht, Josiah's partner in the shoe repair shop. After giving it some thought, Mr. Douglass formulated a plan. He would use the underground railroad in reverse, requesting the railroad conductors to carry the letter to its ultimate destination, the Howell Plantation in Loudon County, Virginia. Here is what he wrote to Emily Howell:

Dear Miss Howell,

I am a friend of both Josiah De Mornay and Simon Albrecht, and I have news concerning Josiah. Josiah told me that he was a servant at your father's plantation and that his mother continues at the plantation as a housekeeper.

I am writing to you to tell you that Josiah was serving with the 54th Massachusetts Division, which attempted unsuccessfully to recapture Fort Wagner near Charleston. In the battle, Josiah was injured and taken as a prisoner-of-war. The Confederate Army intends to either return Josiah to his proper master or sell him on the auction block. I was hoping for the sake of both Josiah and his mother, that your family would try to reclaim Josiah. Unfortunately, I do not know where Josiah is being held captive, but perhaps you can find out this information through one of your many contacts within the Confederate Army.

It is important that you act quickly in your attempt to bring Josiah home. If he attempts to escape his confinement, he would be shot dead without a second thought. And if he proves to be an unpleasant servant, he will be executed, as many of his fellow soldiers already have been.

Respectfully, your servant,

Frederick Douglass

Emily was puzzled over the letter from a man named Frederick Douglass – a name that was vaguely familiar for some reason. Early that morning a man who appeared to be a Methodist preacher, dressed in black, had hand-delivered the letter to her. Now she sat in the parlor to read the letter. The letter described Josiah's situation, and tears immediately streamed down her face. Mrs. De Mornay was watching her and stood beside her asking, "Miss Emily, whatever is wrong? Why do you cry?"

Emily hugged Mrs. De Mornay and led her to the sofa, "Oh, Mrs. De Mornay, the letter is about Josiah. The Confederate Army is holding him as a prisoner of war. He was a soldier in the all-black regiment from Massachusetts and was captured during the attack on Fort Wagner in Charleston."

Mrs. De Mornay brought her two hands to her face and suppressed a scream. Before she could say anything, Emily quickly added, "This means that Josiah is alive, and we will see him again."

"Oh, I surely hope so, child! But what are the Confederates gonna do with him? That's what I want to know."

"I think the Army will either sell him on auction or try to return him to his original master. I must find out where he is being held and where the auction will be held."

The next day, Emily received another letter; this time through the Confederate Army. Captain Beauregard Hammer, had been released from the Union Army hospital and was being shipped home in exchange for a wounded Union officer, also an amputee. Emily was leaping about the parlor in joy at the thought of Beauregard's return.

Mrs. De Mornay had some advice for Emily, "Now Miss Emily, you must remember that your young man is still recovering and sometimes will be in pain. Ah have heard about these things, dear. And you must not go too fast. He's probably still learning how to use his crutches. Be gentle and loving; never let him doubt that you missed him and love him! But let him set the pace for getting reacquainted."

"Thank you for your advice! I shall keep it in mind. Beau says he will be delivered to town on a stagecoach in the next day or two, according to his letter. Perhaps he will know how to find out where Josiah is and how we might bring him home!"

"Miss Emily, I have something important to tell you. Can we sit down on the sofa for a spell?" So, they sat down, and Emily wondered why such a serious turn to their conversation.

"Miss Emily, I must ask you to try especially hard to find my son Josiah. You see, Josiah is not just my son, he is also your brother, actually half-brother."

"What!!! You mean that my father had relations with you? Oh my gosh, did he force himself on you?!"

Mrs. De Mornay, not wanting to sully Emily's memory of her father, lied about what happened that night. With tears streaming down her cheeks, she said, "No, child. I…flirted with him for weeks with the intention of bedding him. You see, I wanted this position of housekeeper…I wanted out of the hot and grimy fieldwork. I thought I could force him to hire me as the housekeeper just to keep my mouth shut about his infidelity. Then, one day, after six weeks of me flirting with him, your mother took you, a toddler of two years, with her as she visited her sister in Washington City. It was then that your father called me into the house and led me by the hand to the guest bedroom. Well, you can imagine what happened next."

"Miss Emily, I was barely eighteen years old when all this happened. I was young and foolish, self-seeking, and ambitious. I am so sorry!"

Emily just sat there looking out into space, not knowing what to say or how to feel. "Did my mother ever find out the truth about Josiah?"

"No, that was kept secret from her. Neither your father nor I wanted to hurt your mother. You know, Miss Emily, I will always love your mother for all the kindness she has shown me through the years."

"So, Josiah is my brother, the son of my father. I always thought he resembled my father but thought of it as a strange coincidence, nothing more."

"Well, now you know why it is important to both of us to get Josiah home safe and sound!"

Josiah woke up from a troubled sleep on the ground. He had no bedroll or blanket, and he was stiff and achy. His head still hurt, and he stood up awkwardly. "Say, do they ever feed us here?"

The man with his arm in a makeshift sling said, "Now dat's a good sign dat you is hungry. You done missed the mornin meal – but don't worry, dey come back this afternoon with what dey call food."

Josiah looked around the large pen. "There seems to be fewer men in this pen today."

"Yeah – the crowd is thinning out alright. Now listen up here cause you need to understand this – there are four types of brothers in here. The first type is healthy but with a broken spirit. Johnny Reb thinks these darkies are ready to be returned to slavery. Dese brothers will be sold on the auction block. Then there's the prisoners with injuries they expect to heal. Once they get stronger, they'll be auctioned off. The third type of prisoner is healthy but shows a lot of anger. Figurin dat dese fellows will never settle down as slaves again, Johnny Reb rounds dem up couple times a week, marches dem out to a field and has dem dig dey own graves. Then dey shoot them dead and dey fall into their grave. The fourth type of brother is not healin fast enough, and dey too will be killed. Dat's why, young brother, you gots to look like you be healin, otherwise you be just a burden to the Confederacy, and you'll find yourself bein marched out to dig you own grave."

Josiah looked at the faces of his fellow prisoners of war and saw that they were all nodding in agreement. And Josiah returned to his prayers.

That evening, a young Confederate soldier stopped by the pen holding the prisoners of war.

He called through the gate, "Is there a soldier named Josiah De Mornay here?"

"Yep, he be here alright. What you want with him?" The speaker was the man with his arm in a sling.

"Please tell him that his old friend from Loudon County, Amos Clifton, wants to talk with him."

"Oh, you must be the Johnny Reb who busted him on the head instead of stabbing him with da bayonet!"

"Yes, one and the same."

"Wait a minute, ah'll go wake him up."

Moments later, Josiah shuffled up to the gate. "Amos! Man, it's good to see you! I guess I should thank you for not stabbing me…"

"It seemed like the better choice at the time. Here, I brought you half of my meal. Josiah, I came to tell you that Sergeant Stillwell will be coming here tomorrow to choose which of you fellows he can sell on the auction block. You gotta look healthy and stand up straight and look strong. Be sure not to look sullen or angry. Smile and act like you would be eager to serve. Oh, I just hate telling you this, but if you are not fit to be sold, they will probably kill you!"

"Being a slave again is better'n than being dead!"

"And it ain't a life sentence." Then, in a whisper, "The Yankees are gonna win this war, and you will be set free. It's just a matter of time."

Just as Amos had indicated, Sergeant Stillwell came the next morning and selected five men for the auction block, including Josiah.

The Reverend Mr. Cephas Calhoun and his wife, Dorcas came to the auction with the hope of finding a young man who was knowledgeable and skillful with horses. Cephas Calhoun had just inherited his late brother's estate in Culpeper, where he had been raising horses.

Dorcas drew her husband's attention to the young man in the middle of the line-up, "Cephas,

let's talk to that young man in the middle. With his light complexion, he is probably very intelligent."

"Oh, yes – that is probably true. The light complexion indicates significant Caucasian blood, and with it, superior intelligence. Let's talk with him and find out what skills he has."

Mrs. Calhoun, an attractive woman of thirty-five years, went up to Josiah, smiling seductively, and said, "What is your name young man, and where did you grow up?"

"Mam, my name is Josiah De Mornay and I grew up on a plantation near Middleburg, Virginia."

"Middleburg? That is in horse country! Son, what kind of work did you do on the plantation?" asked Cephas Calhoun, a fifty-eight-year-old man now slowing down and hoping to find a young man to pick up much of his work.

"Well, I worked with horses, training them to respond to a rider's commands, to pull a carriage, and other duties. And I trained the big draft horses for farm work. I also became skillful in shoeing horses. And I took care of all the grooming and feeding of the horses."

"Young man, are your parents still with us? They haven't passed on to be with Jesus, have they?"

"I never knew my father, so I can't say; but my mother is still alive and serving as the housekeeper for the Howell family."

"Well, son if you come to work with us, we can allow you some days off so that you can visit your mother," said Cephas. "And Sunday is the Lord's Day. We won't have you work on the Sabbath. You are a Christian, are you not?"

"Yes sir, I am a Christian," Josiah could now say with confidence.

As they moved away from the platform holding the "stock" to auctioned, Dorcas said to her husband,

"Cephas, dear – we could not ask for a better young man than Josiah. Let's make sure we make the highest bid."

Cephas Calhoun did indeed make the highest bid, and Josiah began the long drive to their home in their luxurious carriage. The distance was 480 miles and would require twelve days at five miles per hour. This was assuming eight hours of driving time each day. The Calhouns could stay at inns along the route, but as a black slave, Josiah usually spent the night in the horse barn. At the end of the first day, Mrs. Calhoun came carrying a bundle of clothing to where Josiah was making his bed for the night. "Josiah dear, I want you to change out of that horrible, wretched Yankee uniform and put on these clothes. But first, go wash yourself in the creek. Here is some lye soap and a towel."

Mrs. Calhoun watched as Josiah gathered up his soap, towel, and a change of clothing then began the 30-yard walk to the creek. He was carrying a lantern, and she could see him undressing. For a moment, she was tempted to get closer for a better look. But then she told herself, Not here, not now.

In the late afternoon of the 12th day, the carriage finally arrived at the Calhoun horse farm. They grew their own hay for the horses and had a garden for vegetables, berries, and herbs and spices. The farm also had pigs for meat and cows for milk. A black woman named Matilda, about twenty-four years old, was the gardener.

Dorcas called out to Matilda from the carriage, "Matilda, I want you to meet Josiah, who is going to live with us now. He will be in charge of all aspects of the work with horses. He will start this evening with the two horses who pulled our carriage. But for right now, I want you to show him his cabin and the servants' washhouse."

"Pleased to meet you, Mr. Josiah. After you take dem horses to dey stalls, you come back to me here, and Ah'll show you around the premises."

When Josiah returned, he found Matilda leaning on a hoe. She looked up at him with some disdain and said, "Well, you sho took your time, Mr. Josiah. The only slaves that can afford to be slow and lazy are dem darkies you see in the hayfields. Then looking at him appraisingly, Naomi said, "But you is almost white – your daddy musta been a white man and your momma a mulatto. Ah'll warn you right now – Ah seen how Massa's wife be looking at you with a gleam in her eye. She be planning somethin, Ah knowed it. Massa Calhoun be her third husband – the first two died of natural causes. Well, there ain't nothing more natural than a sixty-year-old man breakin his neck fallin down da stairs, Ah'm just sayin. You better watch yourself cause she gonna try her womanly wiles on you. She getting older and dese old men she married never give her a baby. Maybe she have old Massa Calhoun first, den go for you. The baby will be yours, but the old fool will think it be his!"

The more Josiah thought about Mrs. Calhoun scheming to have relations with him, the more nervous Josiah became. This terrible war had to end soon, and he would be free to go. But what was soon? Another year? Another two years? Could he ward off Mrs. Calhoun that long?

He didn't have to wait long for Mrs. Calhoun to make her move. Two days passed, and he was fast asleep in his bed when he felt someone climb into his bed with him. He felt a hand slide down his waist into his private region. He tried to scramble out of the bed, but the hand had a tight grip on him. His response was immediate arousal. In quick succession, his visitor was on top of him, and the dirty business was over before he could defend himself. As she finished, the visitor whispered, "Thank you, sweet boy," and fled the cabin.

The next morning, he was sitting at the picnic table, picking at his breakfast, when Naomi came and sat across from him. She made a point of sniffing the air and then with a coy smile, she said, "I smell Massa's wife's perfume on you! I told you what would happen! You keep that up and you will be a daddy befo you know it!"

Josiah was shocked that she could tell so easily what had happened the night before, and he became terrified of his sin being discovered by Mr. Calhoun. He was at risk of being brutally whipped or being sold down south where a slave's lifespan could be severely curtailed. Today, he would have to be careful not to let Mr. Calhoun catch an incriminating whiff of his wife's perfume. Then, he must escape the Calhoun plantation as soon as possible. He knew that the Howell plantation was about fifty miles to the northeast, his mother would hide him there. If he traveled at night, he might be able to traverse twenty or so miles in ten hours of darkness. But what would he do about food and water?

Matilda seemed to be reading his thoughts, "Josiah, if you be thinkin of escaping this situation, Ah'll help you."

"I will need some food in a sack and a canteen. Then at the darkest point of the night, I will sneak out of here!"

"Well then, Ah'll pack you up some food and water this evening. Where will you be headin?"

"I'm not going to say – the less you know, the better it will be for both of us."

"Ah'm kinda sorry I can't escape with you, but I got a man who loves me on the plantation south of here. We'll get married once this war be over and we be free. Then we go out west."

CHAPTER TWENTY-ONE

Late in the afternoon, after two days had passed, Emily heard a team of horses pulling a wagon drive up their mansion's circular drive. Emily rushed to the window and saw that it was a stagecoach, not a wagon. She felt her heart leap as she realized it must be Beauregard back from the war. She called out excitedly for Mrs. De Mornay, "Mrs. De Mornay, it is Beauregard – he has returned home!"

She watched with some initial horror as the young man tried awkwardly to disembark from the coach. Old Tiberius had been nearby and ran up to help Beau get down from the coach and get set up with his crutches.

"Here you go, Massa. Ah will get your bags – dey be on the roof, sir?"

"Yes, just one – it's the big footlocker. Careful now as you pull it down because it is heavy."

Tiberius, though well into his sixties, still had the strength of a young man. Nevertheless, he grunted as he pulled down the big footlocker.

Emily came running out to the coach and nearly knocked Beau to the ground as she hugged him.

"Whoa, now! Let's get me seated on the divan in the parlor before we embrace!"

"Oh yes, of course!"

"Miss Emily, let me get y'all some lemonade. Welcome home, Massa Beauregard!"

"Thank you, Ma'am. It's good to be home!"

At this point, Emily looked up and saw her mother descending the staircase. It was rare for her to leave her sitting room since receiving word of her husband's death. "Mother, Beau has returned!"

"Beau struggled to stand up as Mrs. Howell made her way over to the divan where Emily and Beau were sitting. When she got just a few feet away, she rushed to hug Beau and he was knocked off balance but landed on the divan. "Oh, Beau! I am so sorry," and she plopped down on the divan next to him. Then she pressed in to hug him and burst into tears.

"Mother Howell, please don't despair! Everything will work out according to God's plan."

"Was it God's plan to take my husband's life and take your leg and cripple you?"

Beauregard didn't know what to say and just looked to Emily to see if she had a response.

As it turns out, she did, "Mother, soldiers being wounded or killed in battle is the natural consequence of war, and war is what happens when men in their anger cannot engage in rational discussion to work out their differences. That boatload of hot-headed South Carolinians started this war by firing on Fort Sumter, and both North and South have suffered terribly as a consequence."

In a small voice, Mother said, "I see, and I am compelled to agree. We brought this war down on ourselves because of our sinful nature." After saying this, she returned up the stairs to her room.

After her mother was out of earshot, Emily told Beauregard of her half-brother's predicament. At first, she did not speak of Josiah as her half-brother, just as Mrs. De Mornay's son. Beauregard's response was immediate and shocking. "We must act quickly because the Confederate Army is executing black prisoners-of-war! I must go now to the telegraph office and contact the officer in charge of the prisoners of war at Fort Sumter. We need to tell him that we intended to reinstate Josiah as a servant at Colonel Howell's plantation, where his mother continues to serve as housekeeper. Oh Lord, I hope we are not too late!"

Emily ran out to the porch and called for Tiberius. When he appeared, Emily said, "Tiberius, please prepare the carriage for a quick run to the telegraph office. You will be taking Captain Beauregard so that he can contact the officer in charge of prisoners of war at Fort Sumter. Josiah is being held there and could be in danger of losing his life unless we act immediately!"

"Miss Emily, you know you can count on me – I'll go get dem horses ready right now."

Just then, Beauregard stepped out onto the porch. In his hand, he held a piece of paper with the message he intended to send. "Emily, I'm ready to go. I have my message written down and money for the telegraph operator. Josiah must be like a brother to you growing up here on the plantation together."

"Beau, please don't mention this to my mother, but yesterday, I found out that Josiah actually is my half-brother!"

"Oh my gosh! You mean your father and the housekeeper? OK, I'll keep that information our secret. Emily, I'll do everything in my power to get Josiah back to his mother!"

Three days passed before Emily received a response to her telegraph. The response read: "Josiah De Mornay was returned to his status as a slave one week ago. He was sold via auction to a Reverend Mr. Cephas Calhoun of Culpeper, Virginia."

Emily rushed to find Beauregard in her father's office, inspecting the plantation ledgers. "Good morning, darling. I'm just inspecting your father's books like you asked me to."

"Beau, there will be time for that later. We must try to find Josiah at the home of his new master, a Reverend Mr. Cephas Calhoun of Culpeper, Virginia."

Beauregard replied, "Culpeper is about fifty miles from here, and it will take us nearly two days to travel there by carriage. I'll ask Mr. Tiberius to drive me into Middleburg to see if I can rent a carriage. Your mother might need a carriage while we are gone, and I would not want to inconvenience her by taking her carriage."

"But are you capable of driving a carriage at this stage of your recovery? This seems like it would be a great physical challenge for you!"

"Well, it might be a challenge, but it is something that I feel I must do. You and your brother are in need, and I am willing to help. I will be OK, you'll see."

Josiah escaped before Dorcas Calhoun could try to rape him a second time. That same night he stopped by Matilda's cabin to pick up the food she had packed for him in a canvas bag. When she saw him at her door, she ran up to hug him and handed him the bag. "Try to stay off the road. Dey say that slave catchers be patrollin the roads at night. If there ain't no other way to get past dem, you might have to fight dem, but dey be armed. But dis might discourage dem," she said, handing him a sharpened machete.

Josiah looked at her incredulously, "How did you get this machete?"

"My man left me with this coz he thought the foreman be watchin me with a hungry look. He wanted me to protect myself!"

"But we don't have a foreman here!"

Matilda smiled and said, "Dat's right. But I didn't use this here machete. I used this nice iron skillet instead. Dat man be resting comfortably down by the stream now, almost three years! Old Moses helped me drag him down to the woods by the stream, and there we laid him to rest."

Just then, old Moses shuffled into the cabin after knocking. "Scuze me, folks. But Josiah, I heard you might be starting a journey tonight. Ah thought this might be useful to you."

Moses handed Josiah a canvas bag. Josiah opened it and said, "A bow and a quiver of arrows! How did you get this?"

"Son, I made them mahself – an old Powhattan Injun showed me how. Do you know how to use a bow and arrow?"

"I sure do! I also learned a few things from a Powhattan brave myself."

"Den you is all set for your escape!"

"Thank you both so much! I'll never forget your kindness!"

And so, Josiah made his escape around 11:00 that night. As he was advised, he kept to the cover of the woods. He could see the North Star, so he knew his direction. Fortunately, he did not encounter any slave hunters or any other person of any color, and no bears or wildcats either.

In one especially thick stand of trees, Josiah sought a place a hundred yards from the north-south road where he might sleep. It was sunrise when he found a resting place.

Despite being dog-tired from his overnight hike, Josiah could sleep for only a few hours. He decided to get up at noon and have a light, no-fire breakfast. Afterwards, he decided that he would take his chances traveling in the day so long as he was off the main road. Fortunately, he was able to safely travel for seven hours and made camp at 7:00 PM or thereabouts. After another cold meal – a fire would have given away his position – he turned in for the night. He realized he had changed his pattern and would have to continue his hike in the morning.

Dorcas Calhoun waited until her husband was sound asleep before she wrapped herself in her robe and walked over to Josiah's cabin at the slave quarters. She let herself into the cabin and sat down on his bed. She reached over what she thought was his body but found that this was just a few rolled-up blankets made to look like a sleeping man. Discovering the deception, a flash of rage coursed through her body. Sneak out on me, will he? If he is in that tramp Matilda's bed, I'll have them both flogged in the morning! Dorcas rushed to Matilda's cabin with the intent of confronting the two lovers. But Matilda was sleeping soundly alone in her bed!

Enraged again, Dorcas thought, That lousy, ungrateful boy! I gave him my body for his pleasure, and he dares to run away!

First thing the next morning, Dorcas took the carriage into Culpepper to report a runaway slave to the local sheriff. As she entered the sheriff's station, a man in a weather-beaten Confederate captain's uniform was studying the wanted runaway slaves postings. Seeing this attractive young woman, the man removed his hat and asked if there was any way he might help her, "Ma'am, I am Captain Jude Lawless. I am a law enforcement officer whose duty it is to track down and capture escaped slaves and then return them to their rightful owners. Did you come here this morning, ma'am, to report a runaway slave?"

Dorcas kept her distance from the rather odiferous captain and said, "As a matter of fact, my husband's servant, a young man about 20 years of age, escaped in the night. He is very light skinned, a quadroon, with brown hair. He stands about six feet tall and is athletically built. He goes by the name of Josiah."

The shock of recognition shot through the slave catcher's body. This is that pale nigger that got away from me in Pennsylvania and stole my horses and ruined my guns! I'm gonna hunt down and kill that uppity darkie!

"Ma'am, I'll gladly go and search for your boy and bring him back to you! I've got me two blood hounds that when they pick up his scent, they will lead me straight to him. Would you happen to have any of his clothes or blanket that might still have his scent?"

Dorcas reached into the canvas bag she was carrying and held up a dirty shirt, "Yes, as a matter of fact, I do. And I can tell you his general direction is north to the plantation where his mother still serves near Middleburg. Of course, I am just guessing that he will want to see his mother before he continues north."

"Ma'am, you have given me a lot to go on! My terms are twenty-five percent of his value to you upon safe and sound return. Do we have an agreement?"

The captain held out his filthy hand, and Dorcas looked at it hesitatingly but then clasped it. The captain held onto her hand somewhat longer than he needed to, and she shuddered.

The captain said, "Don't you worry missy, we'll get your boy back!"

"Oh, there are additional men on your team?"

"I wuz referring to my bloodhounds, Fire and Brimstone! Those boys have the nose for this kind of work."

CHAPTER TWENTY-TWO

At dawn, Josiah woke from his slumber deep in the woods when he heard dogs barking. He recognized that noise as coming from hunting dogs as they closed in on their prey. Then he heard a man's voice, "Fire and Brimstone, you already found our nigger!" Peering around a thick tree, Josiah could see that the man was wearing a dirty Confederate uniform and was armed with a revolver and a sawed-off shotgun. Josiah suddenly realized that it was the same slave hunter he had escaped from in Pennsylvania. Oh great! This guy not only hates black folks, he especially hates me if he knows who he has cornered!

"Come on out, you pale nigger, and show yourself! You ain't getting away like you did in Pennsylvania! You have a distinct stink about you that ma dogs picked up right away."

Josiah thought, Oh, road apples! He knows who I am! Weird that he would think that I stink. I hope I never have to smell that unwashed cracker again. Then the slave hunter started firing his gun in Josiah's general direction, missing but not by much.

Josiah realized that he would have to answer the fired shots with arrows, but then he noticed he had left his bow and arrows about twenty feet away from his position. Josiah decided to take a running step and then dive for his bow and quiver. He almost made it to his weapon when a bullet struck him in the thigh. He let out a yelp, which the slave hunter heard.

"Sounds like I wounded you, boy. Now I'm goin to close in for the kill! With this here shotgun, I'm goin to blow your head off! Your mammy won't be able to tell if your stinkin corpse is you or not. Back in Pennsylvania, you cost me my guns and my horses, and we pert near starved to death tied to them trees. Well, after today, we'll call it even!"

The slave hunter punctuated his rant with another shot from his pistol. This time, the bullet grazed Josiah's head. Josiah could not decide which wound hurt more, but he was determined not to give his enemy another opportunity to fire his gun. While the slave hunter reloaded his Navy Colt, Josiah stood up shakily and shot an arrow that struck the slave hunter in the groin.

The slave hunter screamed with pain and then began to shoot wildly in the direction of Josiah, who, by this time, was back behind the thick tree. He tried a second shot, this time knocking the pistol out his enemy's hand, piercing the hand, and becoming lodged in the tree beside the slave hunter. Josiah was amazed at the outcome of his shots – he knew he wasn't skilled enough as an archer to make either shot on purpose.

The slave hunter was bleeding and stuck to a tree, unable to reach his pistol. His shotgun would be ineffective at this range, even if he could shoot it one-handed.

At this point, Emily and Beau pulled up in their rented carriage. Hearing the wailing slave hunter alternating between cries out for mercy from God and the foulest curses Emily had ever heard, they stopped to see if they could render aid. Emily jumped out of the carriage and ran over to the injured man.

"Oh, thank goodness missy, I am an officer of the law and I've been battling with a nigger up on that hill yonder. He's a runaway slave. I must have killed him – I don't hear him no more! Can you gently pull this arrow out of my hand, and get me to a doctor? Don't touch the arrow that's stuck in my.., well, below the belt. I think the doctor should remove that one, so Ah don't lose any necessary parts."

"Well, I can try to help you… You say you were shooting at a runaway slave up there in the trees. Are you sure he wasn't an Indian? Considering that these are Powhattan-style arrows, that would be my conclusion. Can you describe him for me?"

"That boy in the trees was a nigger. He weren't no Injun. He was around nineteen or twenty years old, about six feet tall. One of those pale negroes that must have lots of white blood."

Emily began to worry; what if Josiah had a pass from his new master to visit his mother in Middleburg? With this thought, she ran closer to the woods, where she thought she saw a man lying face down. As she drew nearer to the prone man, she recognized him as Josiah and fell to the ground sobbing, "Josiah, my brother," over his prone body, thinking of him as dead.

In the meantime, the slave hunter started a new rant, "You know, I think those mulattoes, quadroons, and octoroons, all ought be killed at birth! When they grow up, they become the worst kind of nigger. All uppity and full of themselves, but truth be told they never know if they is white or black. They ain't fully accepted in either white or black society, so they become, what's the word -- embittered. And their fathers, the white men who impregnate their slave girls ought to be dragged out and shot dead. They disgust me – livin like kings in their mansions which they never earned. I'd kill them all -- the white race is supreme and must not mix with the lesser races!"

Beau climbed out of the carriage to see if he could help Emily. Then he heard her screaming, "Beau, this slave hunter has killed Josiah! Then, sobbing to herself, "Oh, what will I say to his mother?"

Beau was distressed to hear Emily wailing over her dead brother. And since he had admired Emily's father and had grown close to him during the war, he could not bear what the slave hunter was saying, and in rage he reached down and picked up the slave hunter's pistol. Then, with the gun held in trembling hands, he shot the miscreant in the head. He died instantly. After some hesitation, Beau placed the pistol in the slave hunter's free hand.

Emily nearly fainted as a wave of terror then grief fell upon her. She was kneeling by Josiah, trying to find a pulse, when she heard the shot.

Emily awkwardly scrambled up and called out to Beau, "Beau, have you been shot?"

"No, Emily – I am unharmed. This slave hunter killed himself when he realized the extent of his injuries below the belt!"

Emily called out again, "Josiah is alive, but we need to get him to a doctor right away. He might have a concussion where a bullet grazed his head. He also took a bullet to his thigh. I have applied a tourniquet to his leg wound, but he won't be able to walk without crutches. So, if you come up here, you can help me get him down to the carriage. Do you think you can do that without injuring yourself?"

Emily was elated that Josiah had not died, but she still felt complicit in the killing of the slave hunter, because she didn't quite believe the slave hunter had killed himself. "Vengeance is mine, saith the Lord," kept piercing her foggy mind. Then, shaking off these thoughts, Emily and Beau awkwardly helped Josiah into the back seat of the carriage.

Beau turned the carriage around to return to the Howell mansion. Emily sat on the rear seat of the carriage, washing the blood off Josiah's face and offering him sips from his canteen.

Josiah was slipping in and out of consciousness. "Where am I? Who are you?" Josiah whispered.

"You are in a carriage headed back to the Howell mansion. I am Emily, your sister. We are taking you home to your mother. Where you can be nursed back to health."

"I don't have a sister…wait I have a half-sister! Oh, you are Miss Emily! You came to rescue me?"

"Josiah, you were always so kind to me when we were growing up. I thank the Lord that we came upon you before you were killed. Your mother will be so relieved to have you home in one piece! So, we are hurrying back home as fast as possible."

Late in the evening, the carriage pulled into the circular drive in front of the Howell mansion. Mrs. De Mornay and Tiberius happened to be sitting on the porch. Mrs. De Mornay screamed with joy when she realized Josiah was being returned to her, and then she cried in alarm when she noticed his injured state. Tiberius ran up to the carriage and, seeing Josiah's condition, picked him up as if he were a child. Emily said, "Please take him to the extra bedroom on the first floor, then we must go to Middleburg and fetch the doctor."

"I'll go right now and fetch the doctor, Miss Emily!"

"Thank you, Tiberius!"

An hour and a half later, the physician, Dr. Johnston, examined Josiah. Fearing at first that infection could have set in, he was relieved to find no evidence of this. "What was this wound washed out with?"

"I was generous with the application of Bourbon whiskey," said Beau. "I hope this was the right thing to do."

"Well, young man, that was the appropriate response, an effective practice of field medicine. The alcohol had a disinfectant effect. But now I must dig out the bullet. Fortunately, it is in the fleshy part of the thigh and not near an artery. Now, if you have any whiskey on hand, I ask that you encourage our patient to drink copious amounts of it for pain relief." Seeing the alarm in Josiah's eyes, the doctor said, "Josiah, I will make short business of this operation, take courage -- you will survive this surgery."

By the time the physician finished the surgery, Josiah had fallen asleep. Emily and Mrs. De Mornay hugged each other and settled into chairs that Tiberius brought in from the parlor. It would be a long night.

Waking early the next morning after about twelve hours of sleep, Josiah opened his eyes and saw his mother and Emily sitting on either side of his bed. "Have you been here all night?"

"Yes, we wanted to make sure you were OK. We changed your bandages once during the night, and you didn't even notice. How do you feel now?" asked his mother.

"Other than a terrible headache, a stinging and aching thigh, and a little nausea, I feel pretty good."

Emily and Mrs. De Mornay just looked at each other, gently shaking their heads. Emily said, "Well, it seems that you still have a ways to go in your recovery. For now, we are going to enforce bed rest!"

CHAPTER TWENTY-THREE

Major Winthrop, the head of chaplains, sat back in his chair and stared across his desk at Lt. Simon Albrecht, "You mean to say that when your 90-day enlistment is up in three days that, you intend to return to civilian life?"

"Yes, sir! I plan to return to my position as associate pastor at St. John's Lutheran Church in Waynesburg, Pennsylvania."

"What's the hurry – you have a young lady waiting for you?"

"Yes, sir! We plan to get married when I return!"

"Then may the Lord be with you and bless your marriage!"

"Thank you, sir!"

Simon returned to his tent and packed up his things, which were not much more than a change of uniform and a couple of changes of clothing, a mess kit, and a Bible. Everything fitted easily in an over-the-shoulder haversack. After collecting his pay and signing his discharge papers, he was on his way on foot to his relatives' house where his parents were still staying.

With some tearful goodbyes, the elder Albrechts loaded themselves into the carriage for the short journey to the railroad station, where they would board a passenger train on the Baltimore and Ohio Railroad to Pittsburgh. Their baggage was already loaded and tied down. Simon had already purchased their tickets, and he had written ahead to Mr. Dunleavy to see if he could arrange for a coach to transport his parents and himself to Waynesburg, Pennsylvania where Simon would return to his pastorate.

The wedding of Simon and Gabrielle took place four weeks after Simon's return. As Gabrielle wished, the wedding was conducted as part of the regular Quaker meeting. But there were several members from Simon's Lutheran congregation in attendance, so the benches were unusually full. Afterwards, a potluck dinner was held. The only concessions to the usual American-style wedding were that Gabrielle wore Simon's mother's wedding dress, and at the reception, they had a white wedding cake that a lady from Simon's church insisted on contributing.

The newlyweds settled into a new parsonage built by the men of the congregation. Three days each week, Simon and Gabrielle drove their carriage to the Rowntree farm, where Simon resumed his duties as the "professor." And so, Gabrielle continued to see and interact with her sisters and adoptive parents on a regular basis.

The elder Albrechts opened a shop in Waynesburg that served two purposes. On one side was a shoe repair and leather goods shop run by Johannes Albrecht, and on the other side, separated by a wall, there was a dress shop run by Ingrid Albrecht. It had a full display window. The elder Albrechts lived in an apartment above the shops. Everyone in the Rowntree and Albrecht families was living happy and fulfilled lives. With time, the Albrechts' memories of their losses in the war faded; and then the remaining sadness was replaced by the arrival of twin grandsons.

CHAPTER TWENTY-FOUR

Emily and Josiah were sitting on the porch of the mansion after dinner. Josiah and his mother usually ate in the servants' quarters on the first floor, but this evening, Emily had invited him to have his dinner with her on the porch. She wanted to hear about his experiences during his escape to Canada and his life there. Josiah told her the whole story and he did not dilute it for her, figuring it was a story worth telling. She hung on to every word.

As he finished, Emily said, "Oh my goodness! You encountered slave catchers in Pennsylvania twice, the first time fooling them with your elaborate ruse about being the free manservant to the Reverend Mr. Albrecht. But by the second time they must have seen the "wanted" poster for you and Simon that my father had distributed. This time, the thugs attacked you and knocked out poor Simon. Luckily, two civilized Indian men came first to Simon's aid, then these two gentlemen caught up with the slave catchers and rescued you."

"Yes, and we stayed for some weeks at a Quaker farm run by some very kind people. And Simon met and fell in love with a beautiful farmer's daughter named Gabriella. It took them some time before they both realized they were in love, but Simon answered my letter to him care of the Rowntree family farm and said that they had gotten married."

Emily was all smiles, "Oh, I knew that he would find the right girl! I am so happy for him. She comes from a peace-loving Quaker family?"

"Yes, but the family was not disappointed in him when he joined the Union army as a chaplain because he was doing God's work, as they saw it."

"He certainly was. In fact, I heard from Beau how Simon had ministered to him when he was in the Union hospital tent for Confederate prisoners of war. He ministered to both Union and Confederate soldiers alike. Simon never let on that he was my ex-fiancée, but he figured out who Beau's fiancée was when he mailed Beau's letter addressed to me."

"But what about you, Josiah? You didn't find the love of your life on this trip?"

"Well, maybe I did. I mean, she showed a lot of interest in me before I showed any interest in her."

"What is she like, and how did you meet her?"

"She is something of a tomboy because she's the only girl in a family of five boys, but quite pretty! And she can cook really well!"

"Tell me more about her family."

"They are a family of Christians living on a small farm in northern Ohio. The father is also a wheelwright – in fact, that is how we met him. We had just broken a wheel and did not have the means to fix it when Mr. Clearwater came along in his wagon, which was loaded with wheels! He put on a new wheel to replace the old broken one. Then we followed him home and met the family."

"You still haven't told me much about the girl and her family."

"Well, here is the issue. They appear to be white, but they are half white and half Wyandotte Indian. When the Wyandotte Indians were driven out by the white folk, families like the Clearwaters were allowed to stay because they were Christians and had white blood. Frankly, I am surprised they were as friendly to me as they were when they found out I had Negro blood."

Emily rolled her eyes, then looked at Josiah and said, "I don't think it does anyone any good to define themselves simply on the basis of their race! You are more than your race – don't let your race put limits on who you are and what you can become!"

"Simon has told me that same thing many times! But remember – I was raised as a black slave. I'm still trying to grow out of that experience. You white people don't know, can't know even, what that's like! A man can't just forget who he was and where he came from!"

"I suppose you are right, Josiah. That is something I just can't know firsthand."

Emily looked down at the floor and was silent for thirty seconds; then she began to cry.

"What's wrong, Emily?"

"I witnessed Beau killing a man!" Emily said, sobbing. "I thought that the slave hunter had killed you – I saw you lying there motionless, and I jumped to the conclusion that you were dead.

Beau heard me scream. Beau didn't notice that I was watching when he picked up the slave hunter's gun and shot him in the head. Then he put the gun in his hand to make it look like he took his own life."

Josiah was stunned, speechless. He sat on the steps of the porch, not knowing what he should say or do.

"Since we brought you home, Beau hasn't been himself. He's been sullen and has hardly said a word to me, and he hasn't shown me much affection at all."

"It seems to me that Beau is suffering from a guilty conscience. He is not a killer. In his mind and in his heart, he knows he murdered the slave hunter."

"In his ranting, the wretched slave hunter insulted not only you, saying that racially mixed babies should not be allowed to live, but also their white fathers. He said men like my father – I mean our father – should be dragged out and killed for mixing the races. You see, although Beau didn't know you yet, he knew that I loved you as my brother, and he could see how your mother loved you. Not only that, Beau and our father had grown quite close, serving together. Daddy said in one of his letters that he thought of Beau as the son he never had."

"Well, at least the white son he never had!" Josiah said with some bitterness.

"Oh, I am sorry, Josiah! Daddy could never acknowledge you as his son because that would have likely destroyed his marriage!"

"At least he was never mean to me growing up. But he wasn't a father."

Emily sat next to Josiah on the steps and, put her arm around him and kissed him on the cheek, "I'm sorry, Josiah."

They sat for some minutes on the porch steps, thinking about Beau's sin and the guilt that must be tearing him apart. "Say, Emily – didn't you tell me that Beau was raised Catholic?"

"Yes, he was. His mother is a French Cajun from New Orleans, and she raised her children in the Catholic faith."

"Well, you know that means that Beau can confess his sin to a priest and be absolved of his guilt."

"And that could relieve him of some of his anguish. That is a good idea, Josiah. You are wise beyond your years."

"Of course, there is still the matter of what the sheriff would do. Would he feel he had to arrest Beau and have him tried for murder?"

"Oh, good Lord! We will just have to pray for a way out of this trouble!"

Beau wisely followed his bride's suggestion and had his confession heard by the local priest. He felt some relief, but the priest told him that he should report the crime to the sheriff. The priest said that he personally would not speak to the sheriff because the confessional is confidential. He would leave the matter to Beau to decide when he should report the crime.

After speaking with Emily, Beau said, "Well, let's just get this over with. Can you come with me tomorrow to the sheriff's office?"

"But Beau, you might have to go to prison!"

"I know, but it is the right and proper thing to do!"

The sheriff looked on with concern when Beau came to his office and announced that he had killed a man, namely, the slave hunter, some months ago. He described the shooting in some detail, including the events leading up to it, without naming the runaway slave who shot the arrows in self-defense.

The sheriff said, "That man's corpse was found by a farmer bringing his produce to market. He reported it to me, and then I rode out there with the undertaker. Son, you did not kill that man; he had already bled out from the arrow that pierced his ball sack (excuse me, Miss) and then severed his femoral artery. He would never have survived, even if the doctor had been there to tend to his wound. We saw the pistol in his hand and figured he killed himself to end his suffering. So, I ruled it as a suicide. And it will stay a suicide because I don't have time or heart for all the paperwork that would be involved in prosecuting this case. If your priest has absolved you, who am I to arrest you and prosecute you? Son, go home and put this incident behind you. Marry this pretty girl, and get on with your life!"

Beau and Emily were relieved by the sheriff's decision, and they did what he recommended. They were married in July 1864, and Beau served as the manager of the Howell plantation as well as his mother's plantation in southern Virginia.

CHAPTER TWENTY-FIVE

Tiberius practically ran up the stairs to the porch where Josiah was conversing with Beauregard, waving the Richmond Examiner printed on April 10, 1865. "Excuse me for interuptin, but Ah think this here paper has important news about the war! Ah picked up a copy while Ah was in town just as you aksed, Massa Beauregard. Could it be true? Did General Lee surrender to General Grant? Does that mean the war be over and done with?"

"Well, that would be important news, Tiberius. Please hand me the newspaper and I'll read the article aloud for us."

"Oh, yes, Massa! Here it is!"

Beau read the article aloud and concluded in his own words, "Yes, Robert E. Lee surrendered To General U.S. Grant on April 9 at a village called Appomattox Courthouse, Virginia. Grant and his Union forces prevented Lee from leading his army south to North Carolina. Grant did not take General Lee prisoner, as Lee assumed he would, and he showed some empathy for the Confederate troops and allowed them to keep their horses and mules, which they had provided the CSA Army themselves. This surrender does not mean that the war is over – some generals will want to keep fighting, and it might be months before the remaining generals surrender. But this is surely the beginning of the end!"

"Oh, when will Ah finally be free?

"Tiberius, Mrs. Howell can sign your writ of manumission at any time. But she still needs your services. Perhaps there is a way we can pay you for your labors…this is something we will have to decide for every colored servant on this plantation in the near future."

"Oh, do please talk with Mrs. Howell, suh! Ah, pray for the day when Ah is free!"

After Tiberius walked away, Emily came out of the house and said, "I could not help but overhear your conversation with Tiberius. Let's discuss this issue with Mother soon. But there is a more pressing issue – through the underground railroad, a Methodist preacher delivered this letter from a Miss Justine Clearwater addressed to you, Josiah! I think you should read this letter right now because we might have to make some travel plans!"

"Travel plans?"

"Yes, well, first read this letter from your sweetheart, Justine! Is she eagerly awaiting your return?"

Josiah hesitated for a few seconds before taking the letter from Emily's hand. He opened it slowly, too slowly for Emily's liking.

"Josiah, pick up the pace here! I'm dying to find out what she says."

"OK, Emily, just hold your horses! I want to read this letter silently first. Then I'll tell you what she says."

Emily folded her arms, starting to pout, but then shook it off when Josiah said, "OK, here is what she said. She wants us to pick up where we left off. We had discussed marriage (actually, it was Justine and her parents who talked about this possibility), and now, with the war ending, she wants me to return to Ohio and make a decision one way or the other. She says that there hasn't been any other man in her life since I left for Massachusetts. OK, so what do I do?"

Emily grew impatient and said, "You know what you should do! This afternoon, you are going to send her a letter saying that you love her (don't look at me that way, I can tell how you feel) and that you will be traveling by train from Washington City to Ohio as soon as you can, probably in the next couple of weeks. Beau and I will take you to the train station in the carriage and make sure you get on the train."

"But I don't have any fancy clothes anymore – just this homespun farmer's outfit."

"You are probably the same size as our father, so you can have some of his nicer clothes and shoes. But before we pack you up and take you to the train station, you need to discuss your plans with your mother."

Mrs. DeMornay happened to walk up to them at this point and said, "What plans do you need to discuss with me?"

Emily responded first, "Josiah will be traveling to Ohio soon to discuss marriage with that girl he met when he was traveling to Canada." This prompted a somewhat annoyed look from Josiah.

"Josiah, honey, Miss Emily - your sister is just happy for you, and wants you to enjoy the blessings of marriage."

"Well, I just wish she would let me speak for myself sometimes!"

"Oh, I am sorry, Josiah!"

"I can see that you two are behaving like brother and sister now. That's a good thing."

"Well, mother, Justine Clearwater wants me to visit her so that we can figure out if we should get married. I have to admit she is really pretty, and she is a nice, accepting sort of person. She doesn't care that I was a slave or that I have Negro blood. She just seems to love me the way I am. Her parents are real accepting, too, and they have even built a nice cabin for us on their farm. They told me that I should consider branching out and begin making other leather goods for sale, like saddles, saddle bags, harnesses, and other items that folks need."

"Son, she sounds like a really nice girl from a good Christian family, from what you told me earlier. I think you should write her a letter now and begin planning your trip! And that means trying on Mr. Howell's clothes so that I can alter them if need be."

"But you realize that the Clearwaters will expect Justine and me to live on their farm. I would not be able to move down south here to be with you."

"Josiah honey, I honestly think that you and your bride would have a better life up north. White folks here in Virginia will always want to keep us colored folk in our place. We will always be second-class citizens at best. They won't let us vote in their elections, they won't let our children attend school with white children, they'll bar us from their colleges, and they'll prevent us from advancing ourselves through good jobs and occupations. Your children will be known as the offspring of a former slave, and I don't think it will get any better for their children, your grandchildren. Son, you will be far better off up north passing as white. You can do that because you are mostly white, after all. And I can't, and I won't come to live with you because I look like a colored woman and would ruin things for you. You should never let it be known that your mother is a colored woman!"

"Mother, why should I be ashamed of my Negro heritage?! My generation is going to accomplish great things and earn the respect of white people."

"That remains to be seen because your generation will have to succeed despite many obstacles imposed by prejudiced white men. I realize that what I am telling you to do would be a sacrifice. But that is what parents are called to do so that their children will live better lives than their parents!"

Josiah looked away for a few seconds, seemingly focused on some distant object.

"Son, what do you see out there? Are you looking into the future?"

"I am. And one lesson I learned from Simon was from the prophet Jeremiah. The Lord said, 'For I know the plans I have for you, declares the Lord, plans to prosper you and not to harm you, plans to give you hope and a future. Then you will call on me and come and pray to me, and I will listen to you. You will seek me and find me when you seek me with all your heart. I will be found by you, declares the Lord, and will bring you back from captivity.'"

"Oh, I knew Simon was a man of God and wise beyond his years! You learned a lot from him and became a man of God yourself!"

"Yes, Mother! And another thing I learned from Simon was that there are good and kind people in the world of every race who will help others in time of need. I am not worried about being misjudged or mistreated by white people. I don't remember the exact words to this proverb, but it goes something like this, 'Commit your work to the Lord, and your plans will succeed.' And this, 'If God is for us, who can be against us?'"

At this point, Emily, who had been silently listening in, said, "So you are not worried what the future will bring?"

"No, I am not. God brought Simon and me through several trials that I have not shared with you all. I can confidently say, 'God is our refuge and strength, an ever-present help in times of trouble.' Those are words I can live by."

CHAPTER TWENTY-SIX

Beauregard Hammer was talking to Emily and Josiah, "The newspapers say that with the surrender of General Edmund Kirby Smith to Major General Gordon Granger in the Trans-Mississippi Theater on May 26, this terrible war has ended. Now, a period of reconstruction will commence. I am willing to bet that there will be occupying Union troops and more carpetbaggers than you can count flooding the South."

Emily responded, "This would be a good time to travel to Ohio, Josiah. Beau and I will buy you a train ticket and provide some travel money because I know you don't have much of anything. When you are ready, we'll take you by carriage to Union Station in Washington. You will be dressed like a gentleman and take a seat in the passenger car with other white gentlemen and ladies."

"OK, but this will be a deception of sorts because I am not a white gentleman but a former black slave who can pass as white."

"It is just a white lie!" quipped Beauregard.

"Not helpful, Beau! Listen, Josiah – like I've said before, you can't let your race define who you are. It is self-defeating. Keep your racial background to yourself, and don't do or say anything that might ruin what opportunities you might have. Establish yourself as a Christian, as a gentleman, and as a skilled tradesman, and only then, dare to reveal your background."

Still not at peace with hiding his mixed racial heritage, Josiah nonetheless caught the westbound train to Columbus, Ohio. Some weeks before he left, he had sent a letter to Justine Clearwater informing her of his expected arrival in Columbus. He would be transferring to a train going north to Toledo. The nearest stop to Marseilles was Marion. Justine wrote back that her father would be waiting with a carriage at the Marion railroad station on the expected day and time of his arrival. It would be about a 10-mile trip to the Clearwater farm.

When Josiah arrived at the Clearwater farm, Justine was waiting for him. When the carriage pulled up, the whole family came out to greet him. Josiah had only a single carpet bag of clothes with him, and Justine led him immediately to the guest cabin, which would become his and then their home if they became man and wife. That clearly was her intention, and with their first passionate kiss, Josiah was persuaded to think likewise – he wanted to marry this girl!

Once inside the cabin, away from the eyes and ears of Justine's family, the two young lovers embraced and sat on his bed, which was now a double bed replacing the twin bed he had slept on during his last visit. Justine looked into Josiah's eyes and said, "Josiah, if you want to marry me, my Uncle Timothy, the Baptist preacher, will be visiting us in two weeks, and he can marry us." Josiah was taken aback by this announcement and, after a few seconds of silence, said, "I need to talk to your father and see if he is willing to allow this marriage! And I'm sure he will want to know how I plan to support you, that is, what kind of work I can do to earn an income."

"A few days ago, when he learned of your visit, my father said that he needed an apprentice wheelwright. The most recent apprentice enlisted in the army in 1864, so Papa has been working alone for the past year."

"What about your brother, Jefferson? Isn't he gonna have his 18th birthday soon?"

"Oh, he helps Papa most days. But in the fall, he is headed to Ohio University to study mechanics and engineering."

"OK, then your father is serious about me becoming his apprentice?"

"He is! But he said that you can continue with your cobbler work as well."

"I'll probably do that once I buy a new set of tools – I left everything with the fellow who took over our shoe repair shop."

"But, Justine, I have something more important to discuss with you. Are you certain that you are not afraid of being perceived as a colored man's wife?"

"Honestly, Josiah, no! Besides, most folks won't immediately think of you as colored. Are you gonna advertise the fact?"

"No, but I'm not going to hide my heritage either. I'm simply gonna work hard and be the best wheelwright or cobbler I can be and be the kind of Christian husband you deserve! I have nothing to be ashamed of and much to be proud of as a mixed-race man. And I will do what I can to help colored people succeed and not have their rights trampled on!"

"I'm proud of you, Josiah, and I'll be at your side all the way!"

"I think that we will do fine if we 'Trust in the Lord with all our hearts and lean not on our own understanding; in all our ways submit to him, and he will make our paths straight.'"

ENDNOTES

[1]   https://www.historynet.com/ely-parker-iroquois-chief-and-union-officer.htm

[1]   History of this engagement can be found at https://www.thenmusa.org/articles/the-54th-massachusetts-infantry-regiment/

[iii]   Union Army officer Major General Gordon Granger, famous for his vital role in the later stages of the Civil War, accepted the surrender of General Edmund Kirby Smith in the Trans-Mississippi Theater. This historic event took place on May 26, 1865, in Galveston, Texas, signifying the end of major Confederate military resistance in the region and serving as one of the final notable moments of the Civil War.